Rockabye Baby

A Missing Child Mystery

Chris Wright

Guild Press of Indiana, Inc.

Guild Press of Indiana, Inc.
10665 Andrade Drive
Zionsville, Indiana 46077
Telephone: 317-733-4175

ISBN 1-57860-098-7
Library of Congress Catalog Card Number 20-01094644

Cover design by Steven D. Armour
Interior and text design by Sheila G. Samson

For Ruth, Janice, and Sharon,
for always believing in me.

Writing this book has been one of the most rewarding and interesting experiences of my life. The journey would not have been possible without the patience and understanding of Rich Pegram, Jacques Natz, and the entire WTHR family. When I first decided to sit out my no-compete in order to join WTHR, I wanted to find a way to highlight the year. I truly enjoyed working alongside Bob Gregory, and I will always look back fondly at that time. But I wanted to make sure that I earmarked the year with a special accomplishment, and this book is the result of that goal.

As a novice author, I desperately needed and was lucky enough to find knowledgeable, experienced, and nurturing hands to guide me. Thanks to Nancy Baxter at Guild Press, who taught me more about writing in six months than I learned in four years of college. Thanks also to Andy Murphy who, in a time of great personal tragedy, guided me through the process from start to finish; and to Sheila Samson, the world's greatest story editor, for turning my jumbled thoughts into something I could be proud of.

Finally, thanks to Sally Jacobs Brown of ATA and Ron Elberger of Bose, McKinney, and Evans, for invaluable advice; and to Patty Spitler, Beth Morosin, and Julie Cooley, for honesty, frankness, and inspiration.

Prologue

July 1999

In the passenger lounge, too brightly lit for so early in the morning, sleepy-eyed first-class passengers and parents pushing strollers began to gravitate toward gate B3. The counter attendant, sipping Starbuck's coffee from a paper cup, had just made the primary boarding call. Other passengers gathered their carry-on luggage and put aside copies of the *Chicago Sun-Times*. They milled about, waiting for row assignments to be called, and attempted to look like they weren't jockeying for a preferred position.

Denise Ryland dumped her half-empty coffee cup into a trash can and lifted the corner of the soft pink blanket covering the stroller to check on her sleeping daughter. The infant screwed up her face in reaction to the bright light. Denise slung her purse over her shoulder, stood, and stretched. She smiled as her husband, Jerry, rubbed her back between her shoulder blades.

"Have you got everything you need, babe?" he asked.

"I think so," she said, glancing at the electronic tickets in the pocket of her purse. "Now, don't forget what I told you," she added, looking him in the eye.

"I know, I know. Wednesday is trash day."

"Yes, that too," she said. "But I was going to remind you to pick up the dry cleaning before you leave. Bring my green dress for the reception." She lifted the baby carrier, and she and Jerry joined the crowd of people drifting toward the gate.

"Oh yeah, the perfect frock for the new millennium wedding from hell. How could I forget?" He made a face.

"Jerry, you know your sister deserves better than that," she said reproachfully.

"Okay, if you say so."

She sighed. "So, do you think this one will last?"

"Probably about as long as the last one, measured in milliseconds."

They walked toward the jetway. The line stopped moving when the ticket agent momentarily stepped away from the podium. Taking advantage of the pause, Jerry set the bag of what he called "baby crap" on the floor and bent over to kiss his daughter Rachel good-bye.

"I'll see you in a few days, pumpkin. You be a good girl for Mommy and Gran."

The eight-week-old, suddenly awake, gave her dad a wide-eyed look, as if she understood him perfectly. Jerry had always thought baby talk was ridiculous until Rachel was born. Denise smiled as she watched him talking to the baby. Then he straightened and gave Denise a long, passionate kiss and patted her gently on her butt.

"Hey, boyfriend, what's that all about?" she asked, gently teasing him in her soft Southern accent.

She had called him "boyfriend" since the day when they had met in the deli at the student union on the campus of University of Memphis, called Memphis State back then. She had ordered chicken salad on toast and he ordered his favorite sandwich—turkey with no mayo on rye. It was the summer before his senior year as a business major, and Denise was in her first year of law school: they were two young African Americans on the road to success. Jerry had struck up a conversation, bemoaning the lack of air conditioning in the building during the summer session.

That simple conversation had expanded into a lifelong love match. Now, here they were at O'Hare airport twelve years later, the girl from Tupelo, Mississippi, and the boy from Anaheim, California, still as in love as ever—even though they still disagreed on sandwich choices.

"I love to hug you, even though that baby thing is in the way. I need to get enough of you to last me for a while," he smiled.

"You mean you didn't this morning?" she whispered with a smile of her own. Before them, people were heading down the long tunnel, disappearing from sight.

Jerry and I have a lot to be thankful for, Denise thought. Financially they were comfortable, and sex was still passionate, still tender and loving, just as it had been before the baby was born. Unlike many marriages where things became routine, almost boring after a while, Denise and Jerry Ryland still found comfort and joy in each other. From their first night together along the banks of the Mississippi River listening to the soulful radio sounds of WDIA, they had always thrilled each other.

"I'm sorry. I can't come until Saturday, but I've got to make that presentation to . . ." Jerry drifted off as he absentmindedly reached for his ever-present and seemingly always-ringing cell phone.

"I know—Beaker Groceries," Denise sighed, as the baby stared at the lights at Gate B3.

Denise didn't realize it, but a lot more was riding on the Beaker presentation than Jerry wanted her to know. His business was slowly going down the tube, disappearing like those people walking down the corridor to the plane, appearing to grow smaller until they went away into nothingness. Jerry was desperately tying to keep his business from slipping into that same void.

Something had temporarily held up the progress of the line and Jerry took advantage of the delay to place a call to his partner to leave a quick voice mail reminder about the upcoming meeting.

"Sorry, hon," he said sliding the phone back into his pocket.

"It's okay," she said, still smiling. "But you already owe me. My spending a week with your family is going to cost you big time."

"I can't believe you talked me into taking a week off work to join you," Jerry said, reaching to take the baby out of the stroller and put her into a baby carrier for the plane trip.

"It will be good for your mom to spend some time with Rachel," she replied. "Besides we can go out and have dinner and see a movie like those couples without kids do. Plus, you know what Gran really wants to do . . ."

"Take the baby to Disneyland," they both said together, as they burst into laughter, picturing a two-month-old baby shaking hands with Donald Duck.

Jerry had grown up in a well-to-do, closely knit family, and had inherited his appreciation of music from his father, a doctor. He had fond memories of his childhood from their family weekends together at Knotts' Berry Farm and their annual trip up to Pasadena for the Rose Bowl. Although his duties on the staff at the Orange County Medical Center kept him busy, Jerry's father always made time for him. In the three years that Jerry was the star halfback on the Orange County High football team, his dad had never missed a game. Jerry hoped he would be as good a parent as his father had been, and wished he had lived long enough to see the baby. Full of vigor, with an outgoing, assertive personality, Jameson Ryland would have made an excellent grandfather had he not fallen victim to a heart attack at the age of fifty-seven on the back nine of one of southern California's finest golf courses.

His mom had come to see Rachel shortly after the baby was born. Like any grandmother, she longed to see Rachel again. She wanted Jerry to come home with his family and she had the perfect excuse—Jerry's sister Monica was getting married again, and Monica wanted her big brother to give away the bride.

Jerry's mom thought it would be good for Denise to get away from lawyering for a while, and loved the thought of holding and diapering this little doll. Denise was as close, if not closer, to Jerry's mom than he was, and since her parents were gone, his mom and sister were Denise's only family, and she loved them dearly.

The agent walked back to the podium and the line began moving again. They were next in line; Denise handed her ticket to the agent and shifted the baby carrier to hold it in front of her so she wouldn't bump it into anything or anyone as she boarded the plane.

Jerry leaned close to her and whispered into her ear. "I think I may take Mommy down to Laguna Beach for an overnight stay soon, and maybe we can get started on a playmate for Rachel. I remember being promised a little football player of my own."

Her eyebrows arched in mock surprise and a delicious shiver tickled down her spine. Leaning across the baby carrier, she kissed him passionately one more time and then started down the jetway.

Denise set Rachel, still sleeping in the carrier, in a window seat in the second row of the first-class cabin. As a well-established attorney used to expense accounts, she had often traveled for business, always first-class. She loved the extra service—a drink as soon as you were seated, slippers for comfort, and warm towels after the well-served meal—and by now she considered going first class a requisite for any flight. Furthermore, now that she had the baby, she needed all the room she could get, and the spacious seats on the Boeing 747 were a big plus.

Denise carefully strapped the seat belt around the baby carrier while trying to steady the baby bag, which was teetering on the arm of her seat and about to spill onto the floor. Miraculously, another set of hands appeared.

"Let me help you with this," a flight attendant said, lifting the bag. "Do you want this under the seat, where you can get to it easily?"

"Oh thank you, yes," Denise said, smiling. "There are just so many things to juggle with a baby."

"I'm happy to help," the attendant said as she slid the bag into place. "May I get you something to drink?"

Denise usually enjoyed a Bloody Mary when she flew, but because she was nursing, she asked for some tea. The attendant returned almost immediately with the drink and a warm croissant and jam. The woman murmured a few words, expressing her wish for Denise to have a pleasant flight, and to please not hesitate to ask if she wanted or needed anything else. The attendant spoke with a warm Southern accent, which Denise found soothing.

As coach-class passengers squeezed through the narrow aisle, jockeying for overhead space for their carry-ons, Denise leisurely sipped her tea and ate the croissant. Turning to the baby carrier in the next seat, she lifted the blanket to check on Rachel. The infant continued to sleep soundly, and Denise considered leaving the blanket off for a while until a passenger standing next to her, still waiting his turn to get to his seat, sneezed and coughed. Thinking that a cold was the last thing the baby needed, Denise replaced the lightweight blanket over Rachel's face, at least until the hubbub in the aisle subsided.

Finally, everyone was seated, and the flight attendants gave their standard safety and exit instructions. Take-off was smooth and steady. Rachel still slept. *She's such a good baby—nothing like I was*, Denise thought. At least that was what Mama had said.

With her caramel complexion, big ponytail, and glasses, Denise had been an absolute terror as a child. When she became angry she would ball up her fists until her knuckles turned almost white, then, red-faced and furious, she would throw the first thing she could get her hands on. Mama had nicknamed her "Hurricane Denise"—a name that stayed with her for life.

The pilot's voice came over the intercom. "Good afternoon, ladies and gentleman, and thank you for flying West Lines Air," he began. As he droned on, Denise tuned him out. After so many flights, she knew the drill. She turned to Rachel again, removing the blanket and pulling the little awning on the carrier down to shield the baby's face from the overhead lights. Rachel rubbed a tiny fist in her eye and mewled a protest at the change. Denise patted the baby's tummy and stroked her face, but Rachel wasn't that easily placated, and the little face puckered. Denise checked her watch: it was six-thirty now, and she'd nursed the baby in the airport lounge just an hour before. Hoping that Rachel could last at least another hour, she held a knuckle against the baby's lips. Satisfied with that, Rachel suckled her mother's finger for a few moments, and then drifted back to dreamland. Denise slipped off her shoes, opened the novel she'd brought, and settled herself in for the four-hour flight to Los Angeles.

A half-hour into the flight, Denise put the book down and closed her eyes. The novel was one of those steamy bad-man versus good-woman books in which some jerk abandons his loyal wife of many years for a young trophy. The ex-wife gets even by becoming the multimillionaire owner of a perfume company while, with the poetic justice requisite in these intrigue romance novels, the evil ex-husband goes bankrupt and bald and his cupie doll gains a nasty attitude and fifty pounds. *Bo-ring*, Denise thought as she dozed off.

After twenty minutes or so, she awakened and again checked on Rachel. Still asleep. Denise considered opening her book again but, to her annoyance, her bladder had other ideas—at times it seemed that hers was the world's smallest. Squirming, she waited for the first-class flight attendant to come by. Finally, she could wait no longer and rang for service.

"Could you watch my baby for me while I go to the restroom?" Denise asked when the attendant appeared. "If I don't get there soon I'm going to explode."

"Of course, I'd be happy to," the woman responded with a wide, friendly smile. Denise quickly unbuckled her seat belt and hurried toward the restroom. The closest one in the front of the plane was occupied. *Damn!* She thought as turned around and quickly headed toward the rear of the plane.

"I guess I'm not the only one who had to go," she said as she walked past the flight attendant again. "I'll be back in a sec."

Luckily, one of the back restrooms was empty. She was in and out in a matter of minutes. Smelling of disinfectant and pink soap, she returned to her seat and tapped the flight attendant on the shoulder.

"Thanks so much. You were a life-saver," Denise said as the two women switched places.

"Oh, it was my pleasure," the attendant responded. "I really enjoyed sitting with your baby. She's absolutely adorable. And so good—not a peep the whole time you were gone."

Denise casually studied the woman as they chatted. Nothing remarkable about her appearance: brown eyes, chin-length brown hair; the name printed on the ID tag fastened to her blouse was ALICE. Her legs beneath the blue uniform skirt were oddly short and stubby and her figure was plump, accentuated by an ample bosom. Denise felt somewhat gratified that women apparently no longer had to look like Barbie dolls to be flight attendants. She was struck by the familiar tone of the woman's speech.

"I couldn't help but notice your accent," she remarked. "Where's home for you?"

"It's a little town called Cullman, Alabama. I'm sure you've never heard of it," the attendant answered.

"Lets see—down I-65 about halfway between Huntsville and Birmingham."

"Oh, my goodness! How in the world did you know that?" Alice exclaimed, seemingly amazed that anyone would know anything about her hometown.

"I'm from Tupelo, Mississippi, so I know the area well," Denise said.

They exchanged a few more words about the smallness of the world these days, and the attendant went back to work. Denise rebuckled her seat belt and again checked on Rachel, who continued to sleep. Lifting the little awning on the carrier, Denise leaned over and kissed her baby's forehead, marveling at the smooth olive skin and tiny round nose. Like many African Americans, Denise and Jerry both had Native Americans in their family trees. Denise's grandmother had been a full-blooded Chickasaw and Rachel had inherited that complexion and features. Combined with thick, curly, dark hair—like Jerry's—the baby was strikingly beautiful.

As if sensing her mother's scrutiny, Rachel squirmed and began to fuss. Denise sighed. She gently lifted Rachel from the carrier and draped the little pink blanket over her shoulder and infant to shield herself from the gaze of attendants and other passengers, and nursed the hungry child.

Forty-five minutes later, with a full tummy and clean diaper, Rachel once more was back in her carrier and drifting back to sleep. Denise turned on her air vent, and the baby swatted at the offending draft. Tucking a little stuffed toy bunny next to the baby, Denise draped the pink blanket over the top of the travel crib to shield Rachel from the cool air.

She picked up her book again, but it was impossible to concentrate on the plot about the dysfunctional and unhappy relationships, and she finally gave up and put the book away. Her thoughts drifted to her own marriage, and what Jerry had said earlier. She knew he loved Rachel, but Denise had had no idea he wanted another baby as much as she did, particularly since he had seemed somewhat distant lately. A few times she had asked him if anything was bothering him, and each time he cut her questions short, saying that he was just preoccupied with things at work. She was relieved that things between them were "right as rain," as her mama would say, and again dozed off, thoughts of a romantic weekend in Laguna Beach and, in time, another baby, lulling her to sleep.

The flight had been smooth and uneventful. The monotony, along with having had such an early departure, had resulted in Denise's sleeping more soundly than she would have imagined on an airplane. Upon awakening, she noticed the passenger sitting across the aisle, a middle-aged woman with dyed red hair styled in an elaborate bouffant, staring at the infant carrier.

"I noticed your baby earlier," she remarked. "She is a lovely child."

Denise thanked her.

"Is that your first child?" the woman continued. "Are you planning to have more children?"

Denise was taken aback by the woman's forwardness.

"I . . . well . . . my baby's only eight weeks old," she stammered.

"I just love babies," the woman gushed, rising from her seat and coming across the aisle. "Let me take just a peek . . ." She reached for the blanket with a hand practically encrusted with diamond rings.

Denise was able to block her. "Please," she said. "She can be so cranky if she's awakened before she's ready. I'd rather not disturb her now."

The woman's disappointment was almost palpable.

"I'm sorry," she said as she resumed her seat. "It's just that I love babies so much. My daughter had a baby girl four months ago."

"How nice," Denise murmured.

"My daughter's baby died. I just want another grandchild so badly . . ."

Stunned, Denise mumbled condolences. The conversation faltered and the woman began to leaf through a magazine. Relieved, Denise turned to look out the window, an ominous chill settling in the pit of her stomach. She resisted the urge to remove Rachel's blanket, not wanting to encourage more contact from the red-haired woman. Instead, she lightly placed her hand on the little shape under the blanket. The baby didn't stir.

Thank God she wasn't a fussy baby, Denise mused, nor one of those screamers who can make even the shortest flight a living hell for everyone on board.

Denise yawned, then stood and stretched her legs by walking a couple of laps up and down the aisle in the first-class compartment, all the while keeping an eye on the red-haired woman. Denise moved Rachel's carrier to the aisle seat, and she herself took the window seat and looked out the window. Sunlight dappled the San Gabriel Mountains below. Denise sighed as she anticipated the coming week. She loved her husband's family, but she knew the time in California would be full of extended conversations, constant care of a jet-lagged baby, and more time than she liked spent watching television talk shows.

The flight attendant called Alice brought her a glass of water with lemon and the current issue of *Martha Stewart Living*. Denise sipped the water and glanced through the magazine. After a few moments she grew drowsy again. *Must be jet lag getting a head start*, she thought, her eyelids fluttering. *I should switch seats with Rachel again, in case that lady across the aisle . . .* The effort seemed too great as the drowsiness overwhelmed her, and she put a protective hand on the infant carrier. *So sleepy . . .*, she thought as she looked out the window to the mountains.

The clacking of unfastening seat belts and clunking of opening overhead storage doors brought Denise out of her sleep. With a start, she realized the plane was on the ground and at the gate. How had she missed the landing? The last thing she remembered was flying over the San Gabriels.

Denise struggled to clear her head—she needed fresh air badly, but as the competitive chaos of passengers gathering their belongings and jockeying for position to disembark began, the aisle was already packed. She would have to wait till the crowd cleared. The door onto the jetway opened and the mass exodus started. Hoping for a break in the stampede, Denise unbuckled the seatbelt holding Rachel's carrier and then lifted the blanket to check the baby.

From somewhere in the distance she heard a woman screaming. As the shrieks intensified, Denise struggled to comprehend what she saw in the baby carrier: instead of her beautiful baby, there was only the stuffed bunny.

Hands gripped her shoulders and arms went tightly around her. She fought to break free, but the arms wouldn't release her. As she slumped in the embrace, she realized that it was she who was screaming.

1

August 1996
Case Number FR006326

"Folks, the average high for this time of year is eighty-two degrees. We've had an eight-day stretch of below normal temps and tomorrow will be another mild day. You can expect highs in the seventies with temps in the upper sixties near the lake. With winds coming from the northwest at ten to fifteen miles per hour, Sunday is going to be a great day to go boating, go get those sloops and motorboats off their mooring and go for it!"

—Tammie Souza, NBC 5 meteorologist

Chicago—the city of big shoulders, the biggest city in middle America—had been in August of 1996 the city with the nation's biggest heartache. Over an eight-month period, four elderly women had been slain, each of them succumbing to multiple savage blows to the head.

The women were of different races and ethnic backgrounds, the common denominator being that they were all grandmothers, and in each case they were murdered while caring for their grandchildren. In one particularly gruesome instance, seventy-eight-year-old Lila Sue O'Malley was found by her three-year-old grandson as she lay in the bathroom, dead in a pool of her own blood. Lila Sue had been prone to nodding off at any given time and the child, innocently believing that his grandmother was sleeping, had curled up in her lifeless arms. He was sound asleep when his parents came home and discovered the horror. Lila Sue had come from Indianapolis to spend a week with her daughter and her family. As she baby-sat while her daughter and son-in-law went out for the evening, the killer had entered the six-bedroom house through a basement window. The house had also been ransacked.

Three days later, Sylvia Czarnecki was murdered. Known as "Mama Sylvia" to practically everyone in her predominately Polish neighborhood, she routinely baby-sat her daughter Marie's three children while Marie attended the Chicago School of Cosmetology during the day and worked the night shift as a waitress at Boy Bill's Pancake House. As with Lila Sue O'Malley, Sylvia had been brutally beaten and the small apartment ransacked. Her body had been discovered by her grandchildren when they came in for supper after playing outside. Mama Sylvia was a devout Catholic, and her funeral mass was attended by many grieving friends, family, and police detectives who scanned the crowd for a possible suspect.

By the time the third victim died, police began to suspect a serial killer. Annie Ruth Wynne was well-known in the black community as an antiviolence activist. Despite being wheel-chair-bound, she had spearheaded her church's campaign against black-on-black crime and was known by every police officer on Chicago's Southside. She often sat in her window with a video camera, recording drug deals and taking down license plate numbers of crack dealers. Annie had twice been commended for single-handedly cutting crime in her neighborhood, and was the poster child for Alderman Davis Burke's anticrime campaign. She was sole guardian of her twelve-year-old granddaughter who lived with her, and who found Annie's battered corpse when she came home from a Girl Scout meeting.

The murder that garnered the most attention, however, was that of Elsie DeBruyn, whose son, James, was a prominent local businessman and owner of DeBruyn's Big and Tall Men's Store. Elsie lived with her son and his family and had been watching their three children while James and his wife attended the Windy City Businessman's Awards Dinner, where he was to be named Businessman of the Year. The oldest child, ten-year-old James Jr., had been awakened by the sound of breaking glass. Thinking his grandmother may have dropped something and might need help, he went to investigate and discovered her lifeless form in the kitchen. The French door to the back garden had been shattered, and Elsie had been beaten with a meat mallet so savagely that the right side of her face and head had been completely destroyed. Young James had called 911, but after that had not spoken another word for six months. When the police arrived, they found the three children huddled in terror in the back of their parents' closet.

The crimes had grabbed the city's attention like no other in recent memory; the *Chicago Tribune* reported that many elderly women were reluctant to have their families visit them for fear of being identified as a grandmother and thereby attracting the killer and becoming a victim.

Panic ensued. In Berwyn, three elderly women, afraid to venture out even to the grocery store, were found near starvation and were rushed to Chicago Central Hospital. In Cicero, the police were on beefed-up, twenty-four-hour patrols to try to find the perpetrator.

The local media coverage was raucous and unrestrained. The national wire services moved in quickly. Few crimes had ever received this much publicity or generated this much paranoia. The search for a suspect had been thorough and intense. Due to the heinous nature of the crimes, Richard Flarigan, the mayor of Chicago, let it be known to the police that an arrest leading to a conviction was a must.

Further complicating matters, despite the huge amount of manpower that had been assigned to the case, little hard evidence had been found to link anyone to the crimes. The fourteen detectives assigned to the special task force investigating the murders had canvassed every pool hall, pawnshop, and neighborhood watering hole and had listened to hundreds of voice mails of well-meaning though useless tips. A reward was posted for information leading to a conviction, and tips poured in: Bobby So-and-So had gone out of his mind playing violent video games; Harry This-or-That got popped on crack and went psycho; or Joey Such-and-Such had been overheard in the Dumpster Bar bragging about how he offed an old broad; and so it went. Undercover cops donned gray, frizzy wigs and floral muumuus and posed as elderly women at shopping malls, grocery stores, and bingo halls in an attempt to smoke out the killer.

Unfortunately, no solid leads came through and pressure to find the murderer and mete swift justice mounted. Recently elected Mayor Flarigan was a short, stocky, balding man with a hard-charging personality who had won on the strength of his tough-on-crime policy. As former chief prosecutor, he had achieved a seventy-three percent conviction rate which made him popular with Chicago voters and had won him the mayor's office by over forty thousand votes. But now he had a huge problem. His hand-picked successor in the prosecutor's office was widely viewed as ineffective, and Flarigan knew that anything short of a conviction in this case would jeopardize his entire administration. Therefore, upon an arrest in the case, he devised a way to shield the prosecutor's office and his administration from public ire in the event of an acquittal or mistrial. Under the guise of showing complete fairness to the defendant, the mayor decided in advance that a special independent prosecutor would try the case. But first, the police department had to bring in the killer.

Just over a year after the first killing took place, Chicago detectives finally got their first solid lead, a serendipitous find coming from an arrest in another case.

In the cold, wet March of 1997, a rash of burglaries had occurred on the city's south side. Solid police work uncovered a pattern: all of the burglaries took place during the day, and all within a ten-block radius. Operating under the assumption that the perpetrator lived in the area, Chicago PD increased their patrols, and undercover police officers were assigned to the case.

Rockabye Baby

After a week of surveillance, Detective Henry Morgenstern, a burly twenty-seven-year veteran who was two months from retirement, was posing undercover as a meter reader for Chicago Power when he spotted a man climbing through a broken window on South Wightman Street. The officer quickly moved into position, called for backup, and waited. Shortly after, the would-be filcher stepped outside the house with a television under one arm and a pillowcase of other goods slung over his shoulder like a perverse Santa.

"Freeze! Chicago PD!" Morgenstern bellowed.

The burglar did a quick mental calculation, balancing his odds of dropping the goods and outrunning a bullet from the Glock pointed at him versus working a deal with the district attorney's office. He opted to stay put and, after dropping the TV and the pillow case, he put his hands behind his head and stood silent and still. At five feet, seven inches, and a gaunt one hundred forty pounds, breaking and entering expert Mike Mowery knew he was no match for his armed adversary. As Mowery was summarily cuffed and read his rights, Morgenstern enjoyed the familiar rush that usually accompanied an arrest—an enjoyment that would be enhanced when it was discovered how this particular collar would key into what had by now been dubbed the "Grandma Murders."

A search of the contents of the pillowcase Mowery had, and subsequently his apartment, confirmed that the string of burglaries had indeed been solved. The common thread was that at each hit the burglar had left behind valuable electronic devices and jewelry and taken only silver, which could be easily converted to cash. Mowery was well known to Chicago PD as a habitual criminal and small-time drug dealer, and this latest arrest was routine. However, this time he had a large chip with which to deal—a tip about the Grandma Murders.

During questioning, Mowery told detectives that during a recent stay in the Cook County lockup for marijuana possession, he'd had a conversation with a man who claimed to have killed the old ladies. Dismiss the charges against him, Mowery slyly bartered, and he'd give a detailed account of the alleged jailhouse confession. The DA was notified, and an agreement was made that if the tip was good, Mowery could walk this time.

The tip seemed indeed to be good, and the police moved on it like lightning, picking up a petty criminal named Jimmy George Hinson. A stubby, five-foot-six, one hundred and fifty-four-pound mess with a constant hack from too many smokes and booze-reddened eyes, Jimmy George, age thirty-one, hardly fit the profile of a serial killer. Nevertheless, armed with a search warrant, the cops went through Jimmy George's apartment and found items from the DeBruyn home. Most incriminating was what was found in the back of Hinson's closet: bloodstained shoes and clothing. Jimmy George was promptly arrested and charged with four counts of murder in the first degree.

The DA's office had hoped for a confession and a quick—and popular—wrap-up to the Grandma Murders, but Jimmy George Hinson denied any involvement in or any knowledge of the crimes. To being a common thief he readily admitted, but what kind of low-life did they think he was, he demanded to know, to suspect that he'd go around whacking a bunch of old broads?

Needless to say, this was the kind of high-profile case that would make or break the career of the specially appointed prosecuting attorney. Since it would also make or break the mayor, Flarigan wanted to be sure just the right prosecutor was chosen and opted to make the selection himself. A number of the best and brightest of Chicago's legal community openly lobbied the mayor's advisory committee for the position. Denise Ryland, of the highly respected law firm of Fisk and Ryan, won the honor.

During her brief career, Denise had forged a reputation for being relentless, both in preparation and in courtroom demeanor, and was known for her "attack" style and win-at-all-cost mentality. Many of her colleagues, both inside and outside the firm, despised Denise's approach, but no one could begrudge her results; she seemed to be unbeatable.

In his first and only meeting with Denise, Mayor Flarigan was brief and direct.

"You know how important this case is. It is to be won at any cost." He strode to the window and gestured to the city below. "The people of Chicago will not tolerate lawlessness and violence, and that message has to be sent to the whole country. Nothing less than a murder one conviction on all four counts will suffice. You come highly recommended by the legal community. I don't want to regret this appointment."

He turned and stared directly into Denise's eyes. She didn't blink.

"I never lose, sir," Denise replied.

"See that you don't," he said, thus terminating the meeting.

Along with the pressure coming from the mayor's office, the public outcry for justice was deafening. Jimmy George Hinson was unable to afford the legal expertise he needed, so a public defender was selected on his behalf. As extra insurance, the mayor exerted his influence to ensure that Jimmy George's legal counsel was barely more than adequate.

Stories abound about attorneys who graduate at the top of their class, serve as clerk for a powerful judge, or head up the Law Review. However, not all attorneys are examples of recognized jurisprudential success, and Megan Schlitzer was one of those. As a law student she had dreamed of spending her career analyzing contracts and negotiating corporate mergers. Unfortunately for her, her intellectual abilities limited her and she had limped through three years of law school. She was nevertheless persistent and managed to pass the bar exam.

The public defender's office is always in need of warm bodies, and Megan was lucky to get a position there. Her shortcomings were quickly recognized, however, and her superiors were careful to make sure that her caseload never exceeded her skills. Most of her days were filled with negotiating plea bargains from misdemeanors to minor felonies, or haggling with attorneys and judges for lower bail for her clients. For three years she'd managed to keep her head above water, but now, having had almost no experience in criminal court, she was assigned to represent the defendant in Chicago's trial of the decade, and the situation threatened to swamp her.

Megan did her best at the initial hearing. She argued Jimmy George's past nonviolent record and lack of resources made him a low risk of flight. But due to the nature of the charges, bail was denied and her client was remanded to the jail until trial.

The state sought the death penalty, and almost nineteen months after the first murder, the trial finally began in the case of the *People vs. Jimmy George Hinson*.

2

August 1997
Case Number FR006326
Cook County Courthouse

"It will be a hot, steamy day in Chicago. Last night on the nine o'clock news we forecast a high temperature of ninety-three degrees. Right now at midday we have a temperature of ninety, seven degrees above the average high of eighty-three, so we are on target for our eleventh ninety-degree day in a row. A strong Bermuda High is stationary off the coast of South Carolina and this is keeping us locked in to a stagnant weather pattern. The typical muggy dog days of mid-July are upon us and Heat Wave '97 will continue through at least the first part of next week."

—Meteorologist Tom Skilling,
Channel 9 News at Midday

Inside the courtroom, it was even hotter for Jimmy George Hinson.

Several legal dogs jumped through hoops, and protesters against the state's death penalty request marched back and forth like a clown parade, all adding to the circus-like atmosphere surrounding the trial. Mayor Flarigan had come under fire from the Board of Alderman for selecting a special prosecutor, and typical Chicago political infighting continued over the selection of "Hurricane" Denise Ryland. Flarigan called a special press conference to explain his administration's position on the issue. CNN dispatched Bill Hemmer; and because Mayor Flarigan's political career would essentially be over if a conviction was not obtained, MSNBC sent Chris Matthews in to broadcast his show, *Hardball*, on location. The spotlight on the trial turned out to be hotter than a scorching Chicago summer heat wave.

The pressure on the special prosecutor was profound. Denise had not been feeling well for the past few weeks, but she chalked it up to stress. She suffered from cramping pains in her abdomen, but shrugged it off, figuring that any discomfort she had paled in comparison to what her opposing counsel was feeling.

In light of Hinson's lengthy (although lackluster) criminal record and the so-called jailhouse confession to Mike Mowery, Megan Schlitzer had recommended to Jimmy George that he enter a plea of guilty to a lesser charge of manslaughter two and throw himself on the mercy of the court, thus hoping he might receive a more lenient sentence. Steadfast in his claims of innocence, however, he would have none of it. Jimmy George repeatedly insisted that he had just happened upon the scene of the DeBruyn murder, but he had not killed Elsie DeBruyn, nor any of the other women. With no choice but to prepare for trial, Megan put together the best case she could, and she and Jimmy George agreed on a defense strategy of his concoction, and with which she reluctantly went along.

Jimmy George had no concrete alibis for the times of the murders. He insisted that the two VCRs and television stolen from the DeBruyn house that were found in his apartment he took because they were simply there for the taking. As for the blood staining his clothing and shoes—well, that had happened when he walked throught the pool of Mrs. DeBruyn's blood as he stole the items.

His trial date was scheduled and Jimmy George was placed under twenty-four-hour guard and on a routine suicide watch, even though he showed no actual signs of being suicidal. He was kept in seclusion and every precaution was taken to ensure that he would be constitutionally and fairly tried, and constitutionally and fairly found guilty.

Assigned to hear the case was Judge Fletcher "Fletch" Barker, a massive boulder of a man with a granite demeanor. He held most other humans—particularly lawyers—in disdain and had no qualms about slapping contempt citations at will. One glance could send even the most aggressive barristers scuttling to the relative safety of their bench tables. Barker was known as a "hanging judge," and there would be no O.J.-type antics in his courtroom.

Jury selection and pretrial motions dragged. Mayor Flarigan kept up via twice-daily progress reports. Besides wanting to make sure there were no screw-ups in the case, he saw the opportunity to have the case expand his political standing into national stature.

This was also the case for reporters to build their careers on, and journalists from Chicago's TV and radio stations jockeyed for position in and out of the courtroom with those from CNN and MSNBC. All of them were on the scene daily offering live updates. In fact, so many live remote vans and antennae filled the street in front of the courthouse that the area began to resemble a monstrous, space-age porcupine. Chicago's Channel 4 began airing a nightly half-hour program in which each day's motions, arguments, witnesses, and questions were painstakingly dissected. The team of Greta Van Susteren-clone Clarissa McKee and Cleveland Demott, a well-known local attorney with the hard-charging, abrasive style of Mike Tyson prosecutor Greg Garrison, offered their opinions and insights. Hundreds of column inches of trial news filled the Chicago papers. Television screens flashed dramatic photos of Jimmy George Hinson, surrounded by guards, being led to and from the courtroom. Crowning touches were sketches from courtroom artists showing angry, and at times, confused, jurors.

Jimmy George Hinson's advocate on television was not his attorney but his sister, LaVergne Hinson Brystadt, a brassy blond with the well-developed biceps and thighs of a long-time weight lifter. LaVergne lamented her little brother's unhappy childhood, his lack of educational success, and his search for love and acceptance, all of which led to his getting into bad company which steered him down the road to ruin. CBS News set up a face-off interview at the local affiliate featuring Denise Ryland, Megan Schlitzer, and LaVergne. What was designed to be a civil sparring match quickly dissolved into a full-fledged verbal slug-fest between Denise and LaVergne, with Megan helplessly and mutely nodding back and forth like a toy dog with its head attached by a spring.

LaVergne, however, was no intellectual heavyweight, and lost the match after Denise's smooth articulation of the people's case.

"Up your briefcase!" was LaVergne's parting shot as she stormed from the set, trailing mike wires and smashing into a cameraman on her way out.

On the first day of the trial, it became evident why Denise Ryland had been chosen as prosecutor. Striking in a slim, navy suit, red silk blouse, and simple gold earrings and bracelet, she presented her case.

"Your Honor," she said, facing the bench, "the people will show how the defendant viciously murdered four women, all defenseless, all elderly, and all whose only error was being in the path of a cold-blooded killer. These women are dead and their murderer sits alive in this room. The people will present concrete evidence that places the defendant at the scene of at least one of the crimes."

Denise walked over to the jury box and looked each juror in the eye as she spoke. "Everyone who has read the newspapers, listened to the radio, and watched television in the past few months is aware of the heinous nature of these crimes. Many of you have mothers and grandmothers who are still alive, who are precious to you. The four mothers and grandmothers in this case have been cruelly wrenched from their loved ones. Equally profound is the impact on the unfortunate children who discovered the brutality inflicted upon the grandmothers who loved them, who nurtured them, who cared for them: children too young to help prevent these atrocious events, and whose emotional well-being has been compromised, if not shattered, forever.

"Four women, supposedly safe in the sanctity of their own homes or the homes of their children, innocently baby-sitting their grandchildren, were killed by that man." Denise pointed to Jimmy George Hinson. "If we are not safe in our own homes," she asked, turning to the jury again, "where can we be safe?" She returned to her seat.

Megan Schlitzer smoothed the skirt of her brown suit as she stood. She realized that she wouldn't make as effective a presentation as Denise Ryland, but was determined to do her best. Taking a deep breath to calm her nerves, she began her approach toward the jury box. Unfortunately, the soles of her new shoes were quite slippery and she stumbled and awkwardly grabbed the railing in front of the jurors to avoid falling. A snickering broke out in the back of the courtroom, promptly quelled by a rap of Judge Barker's gavel. Megan's face burned, and she stood frozen, like a marionette without strings, afraid that her new shoes would betray her again. Once more, she took a deep breath and began her opening statement.

"Your Honor," she said in a shaky voice, "the state, in a rush to quiet negative public opinion, has found a scapegoat for these crimes that I will agree are heinous. But my client is innocent of all charges, and this we will prove."

As she continued, her nervousness grew, and Megan fumbled and faltered. From her presentation, it became clear that she had little if any solid evidence to prove Jimmy George's innocence. Many in the courtroom were left thinking it was likely that Jimmy George would be lucky to get life in prison, and not the death penalty.

Hurricane Denise swept in and demonstrated how she had earned her nickname. She had an uncanny ability to put a complicated case together, and had few scruples about the sources she used to gather evidence, whether it was from information gleaned from a private investigator or a shady back-alley contact. As the trial continued through its third day, Denise laid out a well-planned attack. She went into detail on each murder count, calling on police officers and forensic experts to testify on the crime scenes and to describe each killing in gruesome detail. The testimony of the Cook County Coroner Al Henniman turned out to be the most damning against Jimmy George Hinson.

"All of the victims died as a result of repeated blunt trauma to the head, with the apparent initial blows rendered to the right sides of the victims' heads as they faced their attacker," Henniman stated in response to Denise's query. "Also . . ."

"Yes, Dr. Henniman?"

"Well, in the cases of Sylvia Czarnecki and Annie Ruth Wynne, there was also evidence of strangulation."

"Is there anything else?"

"All of them show extensive bruising, especially on their forearms, indication of defensive injuries sustained as they apparently attempted to shield themselves from their attacker."

"Dr. Henniman, is there any evidence to show any attempt on the part of the victims to fight back?" Denise asked.

"No. There was nothing under the nails, bruising to their hands, nor any other evidence to suggest that the victims attempted to defend themselves, however . . ."

"Yes?"

"There was considerable other trauma to the bodies of the last two victims that indicate they were beaten postmortem."

"You mean, they were further beaten *after* they were dead?"

"That is correct," the coroner answered.

"Wouldn't you say that demonstrates an unusual degree of savagery on the part of the attacker?"

Megan had the presence of mind to interject at this time.

"Objection, calls . . . um, calls for, um, speculation, Your Honor."

Barker sustained the objection, and Denise withdrew the question.

During the coroner's testimony, enlarged photographs of the autopsies and the crime scenes were positioned around the courtroom. In the photos, the battered bodies were positioned like grotesque sculptures. Annie Ruth Wynne's face was a mask of contorted agony, her bent, broken eyeglasses dangling from one ear. Most haunting was the scene of Elsie DeBruyn crumpled at the foot of a staircase, her neck twisted in an obscene angle, the cordless phone lying by her body where her grandson had dropped it after calling 911.

Megan Schlitzer, herself rattled by the photos, cross-examined the coroner only briefly.

"Dr. Henniman," she said. "You state that the victims were struck on the right sides of their heads, correct?"

"Yes, on the right sides, as they faced their attacker. In the cases where they were beaten after death, blows to the backs of their heads were sustained on the left side."

"Does that indicate anything about the attacker, Doctor, such as whether he was right- or left-handed?"

"Yes, it does," Henniman answered. "The attacker evidently was left-handed."

Dr. Henniman was dismissed, and Judge Barker called a recess to allow things to simmer down a bit. The shock to the families of the victims, none of whom had yet seen the graphic depictions of how their loved ones had perished, was overwhelming. James DeBruyn, known from the TV commercials for his business as the always-jolly "Big Jim," had to be helped from the courtroom. Emotions were high and the tension in the courtroom was like an overwound violin string.

The *Chicago Sun-Times* ran an op-ed piece railing against Denise's technique, and even some in the legal profession felt that she was going overboard in her efforts to win a conviction. The senior partners called a meeting with her to be sure that her methods were square. With their approval, and the tacit approval of the mayor, of course, Denise charged on. The more she queried her battery of police experts and witnesses, the more the tide turned against Jimmy George.

All during the proceedings, from the second row of the courtroom, LaVergne Hinson Brystadt dabbed tears from her eyes and fumed and glared at Denise, who occasionally coolly met the woman's gaze, then proceeded to ignore her. Megan Schlitzer's cross-examinations had proved abundantly ineffectual.

When she was through interrogating the first round of witnesses, Denise submitted Jimmy George Hinson's rap sheet as evidence. Over the past sixteen years he had been arrested four times for public intoxication, once for grand theft auto, six times for burglary, twice for attempted robbery, once for simple assault, and five times for aggravated battery. He had served eighteen months in the Calumet City Youth Detention Center, four separate stints in the Cook County Jail, and a three-year stretch at the federal prison in Joliet. Including his juvenile record, he had served more than nine years in the Illinois Corrections System.

Backed up with testimony from a criminal psychologist, Denise presented a portrayal of a man who was a vicious killer with no regard for human life, no conscience, and no sense of right or wrong. Furthermore, he was the son of an alcoholic mother who never was sure of the identity of her children's father—or fathers—and Jimmy George had been raised by a grandmother already embittered by life's harshness and deeply resentful of the added burden of being stuck with the responsibility of her worthless daughter's even more worthless bastard. The old lady had never kept her emotions to herself, and freely expressed her feelings toward the boy, along with frequent whacks with whatever came to hand—fly swatter, broom, or skillet. Skillfully manipulating the story so as not to engender so much as a mote of sympathy for the hapless Jimmy George, Denise wove the fabric of her case so tightly as to leave little, if any, doubt about his guilt. Avid viewers of Court TV were convinced.

On the fourth day of the trial, Denise called Mike Mowery to the stand. Once more, Megan Schlitzer roused herself.

"Your Honor, I object," she said. "The witness is neither reliable nor credible."

"Objection overruled, Ms. Schlitzer," Judge Barker mandated in his deep, authoritative voice. "Don't waste the court's time. This was covered in pretrial motions. The witness will take the stand."

An excited buzz hummed through the courtroom spectators, stirring the judge's ire and activating his gavel.

Mowery took the stand and the oath. His appearance was a far cry from that of his first interview with the police. Denise had seen to it that Mowery was groomed and dressed to clean-cut impeccability, and he now more resembled a stockbroker than a petty criminal.

"For the record, please state your name, sir," Denise began.

"Michael Francis Mowery."

"Mr. Mowery, would you please tell us the nature of your relationship with the defendant?" Denise asked.

"Me and Jimmy George, we was guests of the city a while back, down there in the jail," Mowery nervously mumbled.

A few giggles erupted at Mowery's folksy response.

"Order!" Judge Barker commanded. His dark scowl dared another outburst.

"Had you ever met the defendant before that occasion?" Denise continued.

"No ma'am, I didn't know him before that."

"When you met the defendant, did he appear to be coherent?" Denise asked.

"Sorry ma'am, but I don't know what that means," Mowery said with a confused look on his face.

"Did he appear to be sober?" Denise rephrased.

"Objection, Your Honor!" Megan interjected. "Counsel is asking for a conclusion on the part of the witness."

"Overruled. The witness will answer," Judge Barker replied.

"Yes ma'am, I'd say he was sober. He didn't seem to be high or nothin'," Mowery said.

"Did you have much converstion with the defendant?"

"Yes ma'am, we talked quite a bit. Nothin' much else to do."

"In the course of your conversations, did you ever discuss the so-called Grandma Murders?" Denise asked.

"Yes ma'am, we talked about 'em. Everyone talked about 'em."

"Exactly how did you and Mr. Hinson talk about them?" Denise queried.

"We talked about how bad it was for them old ladies to be gettin' killed."

"And did Mr. Hinson tell you that he had a role in the murders?"

Megan piped up. "Objection on the grounds of hearsay, Your Honor."

"Overruled." Barker glared at her.

"Did the defendant tell you about his having participated in the Grandma Murders?" Denise continued, her voice deliberate.

The whole room was silent, and not so much as a breath stirred. This was, up to now, the most critical moment of the trial. The spectators leaned forward, many on the edges of their seats, and the families of the victims fought for self-control.

LaVergne Hinson Brystadt was obviously distressed. Being female had made her more acceptable to her grandmother, and she also had been old enough to escape most of the abuse handed out by the old lady. Although LaVergne had had to struggle just to make ends meet for herself and had been unable to give as much assistance to Jimmy George while he was growing up as she would have liked, she loved her brother and had done her best to help raise him after their mother's death. She now sat in agony as Denise methodically tightened the net that would either confine Jimmy George to a lifetime sentence or send him to the death chamber.

Mike Mowery took a deep breath and composed his face into his best concerned-citizen expression. He paused for a dramatic moment, realizing the weight of his testimony on the entire case, then replied to Denise's query.

"He told me he done it. He told me he killed all four of them women."

The courtroom erupted into excited murmuring that was promptly quelled by the pounding of Barker's gavel. Denise nodded gravely, smiling inwardly. The time she had spent coaching Mowery on how to respond to her interrogation had been well worthwhile, and she knew the drama of how he presented his testimony would not be lost on the jury, the spectators, or the media.

She received an unanticipated bonus when suddenly, thirty-year-old Warren Czarnecki, a son of the third victim, lunged toward Jimmy George, halted by two bailiffs just inches from reaching the defendant.

"You filthy piece of garbage—you killed my mother! There isn't a jail in the country that will protect you! If you don't get the death penalty I'll kill you myself!" Czarnecki screamed as the bailiffs dragged him from the courtroom.

"There will be order in this court or I will clear the room," Judge Barker bellowed when repeated blows from the gavel failed to quiet the uproar from the spectators and press. The room settled down, and Barker commanded Denise to proceed.

Ready to pounce, like a jungle cat slinking in silently to nail its prey, Denise performed her final maneuvers and methodically began to seal the defendant's fate.

"Jimmy George Hinson told you that he killed all four of the victims. Keeping in mind that you are under oath, is that your testimony?" she asked.

"Yes ma'am," Mowery answered. "He told me he looked 'em in the eye and kept hittin' 'em until they died . . ." Mike Mowery paused for a minute, as though he was forgetting something, then continued. "Oh, yeah—an' then he robbed 'em."

"Did Mr. Hinson give you any indication as to why he chose elderly women with their grandchildren?" she pressed on.

"Objection," Megan said. "This goes to speculation again."

"Overruled," Barker snapped. "One more frivolous interruption from you, Ms. Schlitzer, and I'll cite you for contempt, and you will go to jail!" Megan shrank before the judge's glower, and without bothering to even look toward Mowery, Barker said, "The witness will answer the question."

Mowery cleared his throat, then continued. "He told me they usually had money in their houses, and that he knew them old ladies couldn't fight him off."

"Let me be clear here, Mr. Mowery," Denise said. "Elsie DeBruyn, Sylvia Czarnecki, Lila Sue O'Malley, and Annie Ruth Wynne were all beaten to death. Are you sure Jimmy George Hinson told you he killed these women?" Denise knew she was rounding third base and driving for home plate.

"Yep—I mean, yes, ma'am. Jimmy George told me that he killed each one of 'em."

"For the record, Mr. Mowery, would you please point out the man you know as Jimmy George Hinson?" Denise asked.

"Yes ma'am. That's Jimmy George Hinson right there next to the pretty lady," Mike Mowery said, calmly pointing directly at the defendant's table where Jimmy George sat next to Megan Schlitzer. As he had done each day of the trial, Jimmy George avoided eye contact with the entire courtroom, concentrating instead on scribbling on a legal pad with the pen he kept clutched in his right hand.

"Let the record show that the witness positively identified Jimmy George Hinson as the killer," Denise said. "I have no further questions, Your Honor. Thank you Mr. Mowery." Expressionless, she sat down.

"Your witness, Ms. Schlitzer," Barker said. Megan knew that Mowery's testimony had been damaging to her case, and that her cross-examination could be more damaging. Also, in light of her earlier objections being overruled, she wasn't even sure where to start. Nevertheless, she had to do something. She approached the witness box.

"I have just a few questions for you, Mr. Mowery," Megan began, and took a deep breath.

"Have you ever been convicted of a felony?"

"Well, I . . . um . . ."

"Mr. Mowery, I have documents here that indicate that along with a lengthy arrest record, you have been convicted twice for felonies. Does that sound correct to you?" Megan replied.

"Your Honor, I object, Mr. Mowery is not on trial today," Denise interrupted.

"Your Honor, it speaks to the credibility of the witness," Megan retorted.

"Sustained," Judge Barker said. "Ms. Schlitzer, Mr. Mowery is not on trial and his criminal record is irrelevant in this matter."

Perplexed, but knowing better than to argue, Megan tried a different approach.

"Mr. Mowery, you were in jail at the time you offered information on the murders in question, were you not?" Megan glanced at Denise, who remained still and seemed almost bored with the line of questioning. Another glance at the judge encouraged her.

"Yes, ma'am, I was," Mowery answered.

"Were you offered a deal in exchange for your information?"

"Well, yeah, but . . ."

"In light of your previous convictions, wasn't this more for your convenience, rather than a genuine desire to help solve these murders?"

"Objection, Your Honor—prior record," Denise said.

"Ms. Schlitzer, we have covered that issue already, and you know the ruling," Barker warned.

"I know, Your Honor," Megan said. "But the relevance . . . please?"

Barker tapped his finger against his chin a couple of times as he considered.

"Very well," he said. "I'll allow this. But be careful where this goes."

"Yes, Your Honor," Megan sighed, relieved. She pondered her approach for a moment, then continued.

"So, you did make a deal with the district attorney, in exchange for your information and testimony. Is that correct?"

"Yes, ma'am, but . . ."

"As having two prior felony convictions, weren't you at risk for 'three strikes, you're out' and being sent back to prison as a habitual offender?" Megan was practically giddy, sure that she had nailed this witness.

"Well, ma'am, I was in jail in the drunk tank. I think the worst that woulda happened to me is gettin' in trouble with my parole officer. They wouldn'ta sent me to prison for bein' drunk, I don't think," he said, smiling broadly as laughter rippled through the courtroom.

Barker gaveled the room back to order, and Megan laid out her last card.

"Mr. Mowery, have you ever perjured yourself—lied—in open court?"

Denise began to object but the look in the Judge Barker's eye told her it would be a futile, and she sat back. Mowery hesitated, as if not understanding the question. A glance at Barker's scowl prompted him to answer.

"Yes, ma'am, I have," he mumbled.

"Speak up, Mr. Mowery," the judge snapped. "We don't lip read in this courtroom."

Mowery cleared his throat and answered more audibly. "Yes, ma'am."

"How many times have you lied in open court, Mr. Mowery?" Megan asked.

"I don't know," Mike Mowery answered, his confidence wavering.

"One time? Five times? Ten times?"

"Your Honor, counsel is badgering the witness," Denise objected.

"Overruled, Ms. Ryland. The witness will answer the question," Judge Barker said.

"Mr. Mowery, how many times have you lied in open court?" Megan continued after a brief pause.

"Just once," Mowery said softly. "Just once, ma'am," he said more loudly after a look from Barker. Denise fumed; Mowery hadn't shared this bit of information with her.

"You admit you've lied in open court once before. How can we be sure that you're not lying today?" Megan asked, her confidence growing.

Denise practically licked her lips. One of the primary rules of open court examination is never ask a question that you don't know the answer to. Megan had just broken that rule.

"I'm not lying today, because he told me he did it. I know he did it, just like I know he's sittin' there at that table pretending to be writin' with the wrong hand," Mike Mowery answered.

All eyes turned to Jimmy George Hinson, and the murmuring from the spectators indicated their confusion. Denise remained expressionless, but realized she finally had just the opening she had been waiting for.

"Are there any more questions, Ms. Schlitzer?" Barker asked.

"N-no, Your Honor, um . . ." she stammered.

"The witness is dismissed," Barker stated.

Any attorneys worth their sheepskins know that timing is everything, and when to rest a case is as important as the information presented. Denise knew that time had come.

"Your Honor, at this time, the people rest," Denise said.

3

After four days of listening to Denise Ryland attack and assault Jimmy George Hinson's character and establish the facts as the people saw them, Megan Schlitzer began her defense. Even the most casual observer could tell that Megan was out of her league, and that Jimmy George Hinson was on his way to a sure conviction. Her arguments were inept, and her own expert witnesses did more harm than good. Despite her nervousness and fumbling, though, she was clever enough to portray herself to the jurors as sincere and caring—just the opposite of the cold, calculating Hurricane Denise.

Largely in part to her demeanor, as Megan made her way through Jimmy George's defense, a strange thing began to happen. Some of the jurors and a few of the spectators began to feel somewhat sympathetic toward Jimmy George. This would not do, Denise thought to herself, knowing that consensus would be needed for the jurors to find Jimmy George guilty. Her senses honed sharp by numerous courtroom battles, she studied the jurors' expressions and body language, and noted a mote of doubt creeping in, that maybe Jimmy George was being scapegoated: a petty criminal being tried for a serious crime, and deliberately assigned an incompetent defense attorney to boot. Denise spotted precisely which jurors were softening, and made a mental note to target them in her closing arguments.

Her concerns were laid to rest, however, when, on the second day of the defense phase of the trial, Megan did what most defense attorneys try to avoid at all cost.

"I call Jimmy George Hinson to the stand," Megan stated clearly.

The room hushed. Denise was almost ecstatic, positive that Jimmy George would be such a poor witness that he would almost surely convict himself single-handedly.

Denise knew that in jury trials, it was important for defendants to be able to state their innocence. Nevertheless, it was a huge gamble. Hinson nervously made his way to the witness stand and took the oath. He knew his whole life quite possibly hinged on how he performed in the next few hours.

Megan began her questioning slowly, and somehow, Hinson managed to maintain his composure.

"For the record, please state your full name," Megan began.

"Jimmy George Hinson," the defendant responded, his voice implying a sense of confidence he was lacking.

"Your occupation, please?" Megan asked.

"My last full-time job was as a produce clerk at Burkenstill's Market on South Fulton Street, but they fired me after . . . well, since . . . well, you know . . ." he replied.

His testimony continued for almost two hours as Megan did her best to rebut the evidence that the prosecution had presented. She carefully guided Jimmy George Hinson through the defense they had concocted. Sensing herself the tenuous beginnings of sympathy from the jurors, Megan played up Hinson's unfortunate childhood. She even called on a psychologist of her own choosing, who testified that it was unlikely that Jimmy George would have acted out on a grandmother figure, as he had been terrified of his own grandmother and he continued to be intimidated by elderly women.

In each case, for each murder, she had Jimmy George detail where he had been, stating specific, if uncorroborrated, versions of his own whereabouts. He had either been drunk in the flophouse he called home, or passed out in a crack house; he couldn't remember which, where, or when, and any witnesses there might be were, of course, totally unreliable, even if they could be located. Megan did her best to downplay this critical deficiency, and actually managed to present the case better than most of her critics and even she might have predicted.

As for Jimmy George's being at the scene of the DeBruyn murder and being in possession of the stolen goods, Megan carefully walked him through a detailed accounting of how that came to be. Jimmy George stated that he had been in the area that night, casing it for houses that he might burgle. The neighborhood was upscale, and whatever he might be able to steal would be valuable. While prowling the alley behind the DeBruyn home, he noticed the light from the back of the house and peeked over the fence. He saw the French doors open and his curiosity got the better of him, he said, and he crept through the backyard to the house.

"What did you do then, Mr. Hinson?" Megan asked.

"Well, the house was just open, and I didn't hear nothin', so I went inside."

"Then what?"

"I seen the lady on the floor, all bloody. I knew she was dead, she had to be."

"What was your reaction?"

"It scared me, ma'am," Jimmy George responded. "I never seen nothin' like that before, and it scared me bad."

As Hinson's testimony continued, Denise took notes on a long yellow pad, mapping out her cross-exam strategy. It took all the composure and self-control for which she was famous to keep from squirming in her seat with glee.

Megan's examination of her client continued.

"Mr. Hinson, it's true that you have a lengthy criminal record, correct?"

"Yes, but I haven't really been in trouble for a long time—until now, that is," he answered unhappily.

"Mr. Hinson, my question is: Have you ever been involved in the commission of a violent crime?" Megan asked.

"No ma'am. I've been in fights in bars, and I did some time once for simple assault, but that was in self-defense. Besides he was fifty pounds bigger'n me," Jimmy George answered.

"Mr. Hinson," Megan continued, "you have been accused of four counts of first-degree murder. Are you guilty of these crimes?" Megan asked the question exactly as she and her client had rehearsed many times.

"No ma'am, I didn't kill nobody. Never have, never will," Jimmy replied. "I didn't kill anyone. I'm not guilty of anything like that. Yes, I've made some mistakes, but I served my time and I've paid my debt to society." Hinson's tone and demeanor showed utmost sincerity. "Besides, they was old ladies. No real man would hurt no old lady. That's just wrong."

"Thank you, Mr. Hinson," Megan said, then took a deep breath as she prepared for her next step. She handed a legal pad to the man.

"Mr. Hinson, would you please write your name on this pad?" He did, and she held the pad up for every one in the courtroom to see.

"Let the record show that the defendant, Jimmy George Hinson, signed his name with his right hand," Megan stated with confidence. "As was demonstrated earlier in this trial, by Dr. Henniman, the victims were killed by someone who obviously was left-handed."

Megan ended her examination and confidently returned to her seat at the defendant's table. Denise stated that she had no questions for the defendant at this time, and the judge dismissed Jimmy George Hinson and called for a recess until the next day.

Denise remained unperturbed, her strategy well in line. The mayor, on the other hand, was beside himself. The trial was going on longer than he wanted or expected, and to his mind, Denise was allowing Megan Schlitzer to gain sympathy points for Jimmy George Hinson with the jury. All of his political aspirations beyond his current office were riding on this case, and when interviewed outside his office that evening, his displeasure was obvious. Normally the most media-friendly politician in Chicago, he stormed past the press, stomping on their power-supply cords and angrily blowing cigar smoke in their faces.

That evening, when LaVergne visited him at the jail, Jimmy George Hinson told his sister that he was beginning to feel the first glimmer of hope since this whole sorry mess had started. He expressed some confidence that he wouldn't get the death penalty, and maybe that he'd even be acquitted. LaVergne smiled her encouragement, although when she left to go home, her heart was heavy with a dread she didn't dare share with her brother.

Six days in a sweltering, sticky Chicago courtroom left the city's patience wearing thin and the nation in anxious anticipation. On the final day of the trial, Denise Ryland called Jimmy George Hinson to the stand for her cross-examination; he and everyone else in the courtroom was about to learn how ruthless she could be.

Her brown eyes glittered, ready to use a final bit of information to deliver the coup de grace—information she had but that the defendant and his attorney apparentlly had missed.

"Mr. Hinson," Denise said. "We have shown considerable evidence that links to you at least one of the murders, yet you still deny any involvement."

With the same calm demeanor and blank expression that he had worn since the trial began, Jimmy George once again asserted his innocence.

Denise persisted. "Mr. Hinson we have a sworn statement from one of your cellmates at the Cook County Jail recounting your vivid description of how you killed Elsie DeBruyn and the others."

"Your Honor, I object!" Megan exclaimed. "That's hearsay from a convicted felon—"

"Overruled," said the judge. "Since that witness's testimony has already been accepted, the defendant will answer the question."

Again Jimmy George professed his innocence. "I never told anyone anything like that," he protested. "When Mike Mowerey and me was in jail at the same time, everyone there was talkin' about the murders. All I said was that I'd been at the house of the last one the night it happened, but I never said I killed anyone!"

"Why would you tell anyone you'd been at the scene of such a horrendous crime, Mr. Hinson?" Denise queried.

"Well, it made me seem important at the time, ma'am," Jimmy

George answered. "The other prisoners at the jail, they was real impressed, and givin' me cigarettes just so they could hear the story."

Denise studied him for a moment. "Mr. Hinson, you claim you just happened to be in the neighborhood that night, just passing through, as it were. Is that correct?" Jimmy George agreed.

"And you found the house already open, and you saw no reason to pass up an opportunity to just help yourself to whatever you could get out the door?" Again, Jimmy George mumbled agreement.

"How convenient for you. Didn't having to walk through a pool of blood, literally stepping over the body of the victim while you carried TVs and VCRs out the door, bother you at all?"

"Well, sure it bothered me," Jimmy George answered.

"But not enough keep you from looting the home of a murder victim."

Jimmy George Hinson's discomfort was almost palpable. Denise prepared to tighten the noose.

She switched her tactic, asking a few more seemingly routine and somewhat benign questions, playing the cat with Jimmy George as her mouse. With each answer he relaxed somewhat, but still eyed her warily. Denise found him irritating, but she patiently continued to toy with him; she wanted him to feel as much at ease as possible. She drew out her questioning carefully, noting that as the interrogation persisted, Hinson cleared his throat often, obviously becoming increasingly dry-mouthed and hoarse.

Denise became the soul of concern. "Mr. Hinson, you seem to have a bit of a cough. Would you like a drink of water?"

Thoughtfulness from her caught Hinson completely off-guard. "Yes ma'am, a glass of water would be nice," he answered.

Denise walked to the prosecution table and returned with a glass of water, placing the glass directly in front of him. Her eyes narrowed at he nonchalantly reached for the glass and raised it to his lips. He drank the water and set the glass back down.

"Mr. Hinson, you claim to be right-handed."

Confusion flashed across his face. "Uh, yes, I—"

"Then why did you reach for that glass and pick it up with your left hand?"

Immediately grasping his mistake, Jimmy George Hinson started to his feet, knocking the glass off the railing as he rose. Instinctively, he grabbed for it—with his left hand. The glass struck the floor and shattered, and so did Jimmy George's hopes of avoiding the death penalty. Denise quickly grabbed the pictures taken at the crime scenes and returned to the witness stand, thrusting them before Hinson's face.

"Mr. Hinson why don't you tell us what these pictures have in common?" she demanded.

The pictures of the crime scenes further unnerved him. He didn't know where Denise was headed, but he knew that it was going to be bad for him. Panicked, he sat in mute confusion.

"That's all right, Mr. Hinson. These pictures tell the story," Denise began. "Blunt instrument blows to the head killed each of these women, blows all delivered to the right side of their heads as they faced their attacker—blows delivered to the right side from a left-handed attacker. A left-handed individual such as yourself. Is that correct, Mr. Hinson?"

Hurricane Denise Ryland had reached landfall, and the damage she had inflicted on Jimmy George Hinson's defense was irreparable. She stepped back and stood by the jury box and stared at Jimmy George. Utter silence consumed the courtroom, the only sound being the tapping of Denise's perfectly manicured fingernail on the rail of the jury box. She had accomplished what she set out to do, and knew that Hinson now would crack under the weight of his own guilt.

Jimmy George blinked as if wakening from a deep sleep and looked to Megan for help. Her expression reflected the same helplessness he felt. Denise glared and the judge scowled. Jimmy George looked at the jury box, and saw that whatever sympathy they may have felt earlier was gone. Scanning the courtroom, he saw satisfaction on the faces of the family members of the victims, and contempt and scorn on the part of the rest. His sister was the only oasis of caring in the room.

Surrounded by the horrific photos, what composure he had vanished. "Okay. If that's what you want to hear, fine! I did it! I killed 'em, all four of 'em," he cried, his voice rising to a shriek. Whether he spoke because he knew that he had no way out now, or from simple and simple-minded bravado, no one would ever know, but Jimmy George Hinson had just sealed his own fate in the Perry Mason style courtroom confession. Oddly enough, as he confessed, it was obvious that Hinson enjoyed being in the spotlight. The entire courtroom strained to hear, and the only other sound was LaVergne Brystadt's sobs and cries of protest.

"I knew they had kids in the house and they'd do anything to protect 'em," he boasted. "I killed 'em so I could rob the houses. I never cared about 'em bein' grannies—I never liked mine anyhow."

Chaos erupted in the courtroom. The judge loudly banged his gavel and yelled for order in the courtroom. Reporters fell over themselves in the rush to get outside to their respective news vans, the jurors were thanked for their time and dismissed, and the victims' family members sobbed, cheered, and jeered as Jimmy George Hinson was quickly handcuffed and hustled away.

Defeated, Megan dropped her head and covered her eyes with her hands. As she watched Jimmy George escorted from the courtroom, she saw her career dying before her eyes.

But Jimmy George wasn't finished. "If it's the last thing I do, I'll get you for this!" he yelled over his shoulder at Denise as he was led away. "Mark my words you'll pay! An eye for an eye—" The door slammed behind him.

LaVergne Hinson Brystadt stood quivering, mute with helpless rage, and leveled a hate-filled glare, hot enough to fry an egg, at Denise. She met LaVergne's gaze with an almost unnerving coolness, then swept from the courtroom without so much as a backward glance at the wreckage.

Normally euphoric after a successful prosecution, this time Denise was not in a celebratory mood. Instead of going home, she headed back toward her office through a pouring rain that cast a further pall on her already glum mood.

With the immediacy of modern news reporting, word of the victory in court had reached the office of Fisk and Ryan ahead of Denise. "Way to go, Hurricane!" someone yelled from across the lobby as she entered the office, and a rousing cheer went up as she entered the inner sanctum. Amid all the high fives and congratulations of her fellow attorneys, she quickly retreated to her own quarters. She had a stack of calls to answer. Always another case. Denise sighed and focused on the next task ahead.

She settled behind her desk and turned on the blue Macintosh G4, rolling her chair over to the refrigerator behind her desk to get a soda. As she did, a sharp pain tugged in her abdomen. *Damn, that food was awful at the justice center commissary*, she thought. Still determined to get some work done, she rolled back to her desk. As she popped the top on the soda, a dull ache settled into her belly.

"A damned ulcer—just what I need right now!" she grumbled.

Ignoring the discomfort, she pulled a file for reference and looked through a stack of pink "while you were out" message slips. Deciding to return to them later that night or the next day, she turned to the computer to enter some notes.

Sweat beaded her forehead as the ache in her belly went from dull to sharp. As it intensified, she began to wonder if she'd picked up a case of food poisoning. Whatever it was, it could no longer be ignored, and she decided to call it a day. She exited out of her program and switched the computer off. Not wanting to attract attention as she left the office, she waited a moment, hoping for the pain to subside.

Denise took a deep breath and stood. She felt a pop in her abdomen, then an agony so intense it took her breath away. She realized she wouldn't be able to handle this on her own after all and stumbled across the office. She stepped through the door and, ashen-faced, fell to her knees beside her startled secretary. Blackness engulfed her.

4

A beeping noise awakened Denise, and she tentatively opened her eyes, blinking at the bright light that assaulted them. Raising her hand to rub her eyes, she was startled to find an IV needle and tubing in the back of her hand.

She gazed at her surroundings. Pale blue walls, flowered curtains, a recliner chair near her bed, and flowers. Bouquets and bouquets of flowers.

"Shit," she muttered. "Am I in the hospital?"

Her last clear memory was of the popping in her abdomen and pain that even she, with her gift for articulation, would have trouble describing. Denise vaguely remembered sirens, an ambulance ride, and lots of people in scrub suits and surgical masks hovering over and messing with her, but she had more or less thought that to be part of a bad dream. She shifted in the bed and grimaced, realizing it had been no dream. She fumbled for the call button, and just as she was about to press it Jerry came into the room.

"Hey, baby, welcome back," he said, smiling and taking her hand.

"Jerry," she mumbled. "Where am I?"

"Chicago General, but you're okay," he replied. "You did have me scared for a while, but you're definitely okay now."

"What happened?" Denise asked. "I felt something pop, like appendicitis . . ."

As if in answer to her question, a young doctor came into the room.

"Hi, Mrs. Ryland," he said. "I'm Dr. Fields, surgeon. How are you feeling?"

"I've felt better. Anyone want to tell me why I'm here?"

"I'll be happy to answer all your questions, but let me check you over a bit first."

As he examined her eyes and listened to her chest and heart, she grumpily looked him over. Not exactly young enough to be her son, but definitely young enough to be a nephew of a much-older sister.

"Does your mother know you're here?" she griped to him.

He laughed. "Is she always this feisty?" he asked Jerry.

"You ain't seen nothin', man," came the reply.

Dr. Fields lifted Denise's hospital gown to check her abdomen, and she was shocked to see a white dressing covering it. "Okay, no more dancing around," she said. "Tell me what happened."

"When was the last time you had a physical examination, Mrs. Ryland?" Dr. Fields asked.

"I don't know. I've been so busy lately. Let me think . . . I believe I saw the doctor about a year ago," she lied. She hadn't seen a doctor for at least two years.

He asked her a few more questions. She was tired and still in some pain, and the combination made her cranky and impatient. "I said, I want to know what happened. Are you going to tell me or not?"

Jerry sat down on the bed beside her and rubbed her hand against his face.

"You had a miscarriage, babe," Jerry said quietly, wiping his eyes. "You were six weeks pregnant."

That couldn't be right. There had to be some mistake. She and Jerry had been trying to have a baby for several months now, but she hadn't even missed a period; no way she could have been pregnant. But as she looked at the doctor, who solemnly nodded, and back to her husband, she knew it wasn't a mistake, and the full impact of his words sank in. Tears filled her eyes and slid down her cheeks.

"It was an ectopic—tubal—pregnancy," the doctor said. "Your fallopian tube ruptured, and that's what caused you so much pain." He hurried on, wanting to reassure her. "We performed a laparoscopy. Even though that tube is severely damaged, the other one is in great shape, so I don't expect you'll have any trouble conceiving again."

Denise drew a ragged breath. "I've been working so hard. Did I do something . . . I mean, could I have done anything . . . ?

"No, no, Mrs. Ryland," Dr. Fields answered. "Unfortunately, these things sometimes happen, and there's nothing you can do about it. But when an ectopic pregnancy does occur, it's because the fertilized egg doesn't move on down to the uterus as it's supposed to, and not because of something a woman does or doesn't do. It's just a fluke. Don't blame yourself, because it most definitely wasn't your fault."

She found little consolation in the doctor's words, and her tears continued to well.

From their days on campus, Jerry and Denise had looked forward to the day when they would have children together. She had always cherished the thought of giving Jerry a son to carry on his family's name, a "little football player of his own." The timing never seemed to be right with both of them trying to establish their careers.

The driving effort over the past few years to make partner at Fisk and Ryan had been her number-one priority, the only thing besides her husband that seemed to matter to her. Since her parents had died and she had no brothers or sisters, all she had in the world was her work and Jerry. She hadn't worried about not seeing a doctor for so long since she had stopped taking the pill, and had always figured she would know immediately whenever she became pregnant. The realization that not everything went according to her own schedule now hit her hard, and she realized what her zeal for her career had almost cost. She could have died.

Dr. Fields offered a few more words of encouragement, and with a promise to look in on her later before his shift ended, he left her and Jerry alone.

"Babe, I know you feel terrible right now, but I want you to know that I love you and we'll get through this together," Jerry said, brushing her hair aside and kissing her forehead. He looked so forlorn and sad.

"I'm sorry I let you down, Jerry. I didn't know or I would have taken better care of myself."

"Hey, you heard what the doctor said. It wasn't your fault—it couldn't be helped." He smiled and kissed her fingers. "It's okay. There's nothing else in the world more important to me than you. Your health is what counts. I'm sorry about the baby, you know that, but right now you need to concentrate just on getting better. When the time is right we'll have a houseful."

"Still love me, boyfriend?" Denise asked.

"You know I do. You get some rest, okay? I'll be right here," he said, gesturing toward the recliner.

She smiled and kissed his hand. Then she curled up on her side facing away from him and silently cried herself to sleep.

5

After two more days in the hospital Denise was discharged with stern instructions to do no driving or heavy lifting for two weeks. Bored to distraction by inactivity, She had work sent to her home so she could keep current. Because she was young and healthy, her strength quickly returned and she settled back in her old routine as soon as possible: a five-mile run at five A.M. followed by a quick shower and arrival at the office by seven, where she put in her standard twelve-hour day. It was early September now and she loved the cool morning air. Lunch and dinner were quick, usually take-out from the third-floor deli, eaten at her desk unless business dictated otherwise. Her full day continued until seven in the evening.

Much to the chagrin of some of Denise's colleagues at Fisk and Ryan, even a serious illness and bout in the hospital did nothing to tame the Hurricane. She was back and hungrier than ever. Always intensely private, Denise shared the information about the miscarriage to only those who needed to know. She considered illness a sign of weakness, and weakness was not a trait she felt she could afford to show. Besides, it was no one else's business.

Meanwhile, her work as special prosecutor in the Grandma Murders case had not gone unnoticed. Denise had proved she could perform well under intense public pressure and daily media scrutiny. More important, her success generated extremely valuable publicity for the firm.

A few weeks after she had returned to work, Charles Kenton Fisk, one of the firm's founding partners, invited Denise to lunch at the Golden Hind, one of Chicago's finest restaurants. Denise felt a rush of nerves. Fisk did not lunch with one of the attorneys on staff without good reason. She knew she had assembled enough billable hours to reach from her office to the lake shore. Was it time for the big payoff?

For the luncheon meeting, Denise dressed in a deep red Anne Klein suit and wore her "lucky" pearls, the ones she had bought with her commission from settling the Miller Street Bridge impasse. That had been her first high-profile case, one that proved very profitable for the firm, in which she had brokered a deal that allowed a new strip mall to be built in the Millburgh district. The mall developers wanted the old Miller Street Bridge torn down to improve the flow of traffic to the new shopping area. Denise had to convince the residents, some who had lived in the community twenty years or more, to allow the bridge to be torn down.

At the time, they didn't know that the front of the strip mall, as well as all of its entrances, would be built facing another neighborhood and not their own. They didn't know that there would never be another bridge erected to replace the old one. They also weren't aware of the research that showed their neighborhood, cut off from the main flow of traffic in the area, would slowly die.

Denise knew these facts and withheld that information in order to gain the approval of the neighborhood association. Moreover, a rookie newspaper reporter had uncovered the same information and Denise convinced him not to print the story. With her Southern charm and down-home ways, she could be believable. Denise could charm a 'possum out of a tree, her mama used to say. The bridge was torn down and construction on the mall was well underway before anyone realized her ploy, but by then it was too late. The mall developer made millions, the firm made hundreds of thousands, and Denise didn't do too badly herself.

She soothed her conscience by telling herself that as attorney her objective was to do what was best for her client, no matter what. Still, she wondered what Mama would have thought of her deception. She thought of the little white church on top of Beaker Hill in Tupelo, Mississippi, with all the neighbors sitting in the pews singing "Just A Closer Walk With Thee." Since her walk with Him hadn't been very close lately, she knew that she'd have some fences to mend—someday. But for now she had to arrive at the spot destiny had decreed for her.

Denise had been with the firm for eight years. While it was extremely unusual for the average attorney to make partner with less than ten year's experience, Denise Ryland clearly was not the average attorney. She was not a woman encumbered with children, and she did have an understanding husband. For years she had been the firm's leader in billable hours. With the information she'd received from Dale Romanski, a ferreting detective she often employed, she had been able to achieve victory in some cases in which her position was actually very weak. Denise's father had been a formidable attorney in his own right, and she had inherited his keen legal mind and way of disarming opponents and capitalizing on their weaknesses. Winning the conviction of Jimmy George Hinson in the Grandma Murders case had been the highlight of her career.

The atmosphere became charged when Charles Kenton Fisk entered the restaurant. A tall, striking man with gray hair, craggy but well-groomed with a penchant for five-thousand-dollar suits, he commanded attention. The maitre d' bowed so low in greeting he almost did a headstand. The Golden Hind was Fisk's personal favorite and he often dined there with clients and partners. The headwaiter was ready at hand with two very dry vodka martinis by the time Fisk reached the table. Denise rose to greet her employer, and he shook her hand, nodding for her to sit again.

"Denise, how good of you to come. It's always so nice to see you, and good to see you well and back in the swim again," Fisk said, sipping his martini. He inquired about Jerry.

She told him that Jerry was fine and that everything was going well. She sipped at her own martini; it wasn't her favorite cocktail, but she knew better than to intimate such a thing. It never hurt to drink what the big guys drank.

They ordered their meals, and after a few more pleasantries, Fisk got abruptly to the point.

"Denise, your work with the firm has always been exemplary. The amount of revenue you have engendered in the past eight years has been considerable, of course, and I trust you've been satisfied with your compensation."

Denise murmured her thanks and reassured him that the paychecks and bonuses she had received had been sufficiently generous.

"We always review subordinates' cases each month, to check progress. Particularly of late, your attention to detail, your analytical thinking, and your ability to often salvage a case when there doesn't seem to be much to go on has been outstanding." Fisk leaned back and savored the martini. Denise's gaze was level as he spoke, but she left her drink on the table for fear that her hand would shake, giving away her nervousness.

"Our client load has risen dramatically since the Hinson case," Fisk continued. "I've seen Mayor Flarigan at a couple of banquets since then, and he continues to sing your praises. To say he was impressed with the way you handled that case would be an understatement."

"Thank you, Mr. Fisk," Denise responded. "I'm glad I was able to prove the confidence you and the mayor put into my ability." Her nerves were screaming by now, and only her remarkable self-control kept her from becoming ill.

"Indeed, our confidence in you has always been well founded. You've been a wonderful asset to the firm, just as the other partners and I always thought you'd be. We would like to ensure our continued association in a manner that's most beneficial to all of us, and would like to invite you to become a partner with Fisk and Ryan." He leaned back to study her reaction.

There it was, all out in the open. It was what she had hoped for. It was what she had worked to achieve. She thought back to the days when she was growing up in the South, going to school in the rickety old building where her mama was a teacher, and how tough it had been to be the teacher's daughter. Maybe it wasn't a fancy private school, but she'd received a good education, and now her hard work had all paid off.

"If you can dream it, you can believe it; if you can believe it, you can achieve it," was one of Mama's many aphorisms. A sharecropper's daughter who had grown up in a small but tidy one-room cabin where the rain came through the roof and onto her cot, Mama had been strong on sayings that emphasized the value of dreams, ethics, and good living. She posted them on the blackboard each day and taught them to her students. To Denise it seemed that there was an aphorism for every event, for every occasion, and for every person she'd ever met.

"Mr. Fisk, I don't have to consider your gracious invitation. I'd be honored to become a partner," she said, showing her enthusiasm but fighting to remain calm when she wanted to crow with delight.

"Well, we hoped you would feel that way," he smiled. "Of course, a compensatory package will be arranged for you with the usual perks, and you will move upstairs to a new office."

"Thank you, Mr. Fisk. I'm grateful."

"One more thing, Denise."

"Yes, sir?"

"The partners all call me Kent."

As they ate their lunch and made small talk, Denise considered what had just occurred. There were only five partners in Fisk and Ryan, and she was now the sixth, and the only woman—and an African-American woman at that. She was anxious to share her joy with Jerry, and as soon as lunch was over and she and Fisk parted company—he had another meeting to attend—she called Jerry on her cell phone. He wasn't in his office, and she assumed he was probably having lunch with a client. Jerry often said that the public relations game was just one lunch meeting after another.

When Denise got back to her office, Lisa, her secretary, was waiting with a bottle of champagne. Colleagues came around and offered congratulations and wished her well. If any of them begrudged or resented her promotion, she couldn't tell, nor did she particularly care. She put in an appearance of attending to the work on her desk, but was giddy from the promotion and the champagne, and finally, at four o'clock, Lisa cajoled her into calling it a day and taking the rest of the afternoon off to celebrate. Denise didn't have to be asked twice; she couldn't wait to get home to tell Jerry her good news and celebrate with him.

When she pulled into the driveway, she was gratified to see Jerry's car already there. She called to him as she entered the house.

"Down here, babe," he answered from the basement. Denise shed her jacket, kicked off her shoes, and went to the kitchen and opened a bottle of merlot. She poured two glasses and carried them down to the basement. There, she sat on the stairs and watched him.

At least four nights a week Jerry lifted weights and did flexibility drills, a routine he was able to maintain since Denise often worked late. Always a business-minded man, he usually combined his work with his exercise, and tonight was no different. A videotape of a sales presentation he was working on was playing on the television. She admired his tenacity; his small public relations agency always had to really hustle to compete with the big boys, but somehow, they always managed.

Denise had provided the start-up capital for her husband's business, but it was a move she never had regretted, just as she had never regretted marrying him. She was reminded of what had attracted her to him so many years ago as she gazed at the bulging, rippling muscles as he lifted the weights.

"Lookin' good, boyfriend," she murmured in a low voice.

He finished the set and put the weights down. His thighs flexed as he walked over to pick up a towel to dry his hairy, sweat-drenched body. As he dried his wavy dark hair she felt a flutter of arousal deep in her belly. He wiped his face with the towel and regarded her with a raised eyebrow.

"Hmm, you're home about two hours early, and you've busted into the good wine," he teased. "I sense a cat who's swallowed a sizable canary. What are you up to?"

"What makes you think I'm up to something?" she asked as she handed him a glass. "Can't I come home early and have a glass of wine with my husband without rousing suspicion?"

"Baby, I've known you too long," he said as he slipped his arm around her waist and pulled her to him. "Nothing's wrong, is it?"

"Mmmm, nothing that a little boyfriend time can't fix," she said, grabbing him and kissing him passionately. He didn't know what was going on but it was starting out fine. He pulled away and looked her in the eye.

"Okay now, spill. What's up?" he asked.

"What would you do if I said you were kissing a partner at Fisk and Ryan?"

"For real? Are you serious?"

"Are you surprised?" she asked.

"Babe, nothing you do surprises me. Tell me about it."

They sat on the weight bench and Denise described the luncheon at the Golden Hind, even down to how many olives had been in the martinis. Her eyes sparkled and flashed as she told the story, and Jerry basked in the glow of excitement on her lovely face.

"Congratulations, babe, I knew you could do it. It was just a matter of time," he said.

They stood, and with a whoop he swept her up in his arms and spun her around as she shrieked with delight, just as he'd done in college after he scored the winning touchdown against Ole Miss.

They made love, then finished the wine and grilled steaks for dinner. Their joy seemed almost complete. There had been many good days for them over the nine years they'd been married, and some not-so-good ones as well, but that was part of the for-better-or-worse. They had dated for two years before they married, and even though her friends cautioned her about marrying a man three years younger than she was, she and Jerry had outlasted many of the skeptics. Granted, Denise had always enjoyed more career success than Jerry, but he had never shown any envy or jealousy. The only thing missing was children, Denise thought with a pang. But they were still young, and the doctor had said that there was no reason that parenthood couldn't happen.

6

February 1998
Case Number 007018

> "Good morning. Another windy, bone-chilling day is blowing up for the Windy City. We have a few snow showers in store for today, with little if any accumulation—but is it ever going to be cold! Temperatures will hover in the teens this morning and we'll stay below freezing all day with wind-chill at ten below."
>
> —Lyra O'Brien, Chicagoland TV morning meteorologist

Denise always watched the morning news show to get her day started, and she shook her head as cute, lively Lyra O'Brien, reporting live from the Chicago Cat Show, struggled with a frantic Persian that someone had stuck in her arms and looked like it was ready to undergo a fur explosion. *That girl's suit's shot for the day,* Denise mused as she hit the mute button on the television in her office and sipped a steaming cup of coffee. Even though she was now a partner, she saw no reason to rest on her laurels and continued the same work routine as before, usually putting in twelve-hour days. She'd been in her new corner office for a few weeks, and the other partners frequently popped in the door to consult with her; they also seemed receptive to her input in the partner meetings.

In spite of her achievement, an unfamiliar restlessness had now taken permanent residence in her psyche. She couldn't seem to get past the loss of her baby, and brooded over what could have been if the pregnancy had gone to term.

"Let the dead bury the dead," Mama would have said. Well, Mama had always been a little lacking in the tenderness department. Denise sighed, thinking that maybe things had worked out for the best. Now that she had become a partner, having a child would definitely have to be put on the back burner. *Like mother, like daughter,* she thought.

March of 1998 brought her next big case—an extremely messy one. Daniel Richards, one of Chicago's most powerful attorneys and a friend of the firm, was about to get a divorce. He was a known womanizer. He also was known as one of the top attorneys in the Midwest. With an annual salary of nearly a million dollars, he had a lot to lose. No stranger to the divorce process, as this was his third, he'd had the foresight to arrange a solid prenuptial agreement, but that was actually part of the complications.

The current wife, Linda Richards, a former cocktail waitress he'd met at a bar association banquet, and who was twenty years his junior, was contesting the prenup. After the first three months, the marriage had become as superficial as the bride's face and body, both of which had been built and rebuilt several times since the honeymoon had ended. Rumors also abounded about Mrs. Richards' lack of fidelity, with the chatter saying she had been as open with her favors as a twenty-four-hour convenience store on a Sunday night. Daniel Richards was incensed not so much over that as he was that she was asking for half of the income he had earned during their two-and-a-half-year marriage. He found that totally unacceptable. According to the prenup, she was entitled to less than two hundred thousand dollars. To him, that was a pittance, but the deceitful hussy was demanding more than three times that amount, claiming that *he* had been unfaithful, which voided the contract.

Kent Fisk rarely visited the other offices unless it was absolutely necessary, so Denise knew a big boom was going to be lowered when he came calling on her one afternoon. Attorneys often referred clients with special needs to other firms, and it was crucial to maintain a good working relationship with a man as well-connected as Daniel Richards. Denise was aware that, over the years, Richards' referrals had resulted in hundreds of thousands of dollars in billing for Fisk and Ryan, and Kent Fisk didn't need to point out to her what she already knew—she couldn't blow this one.

"Daniel has found himself in a—how shall I phrase it?—very delicate position, and he needs our help. I trust that you'll be able to give his case special attention."

"Of course, Kent. I'll make it a top priority," she replied.

"Needless to say, the utmost discretion is needed," he continued.

"Absolutely," she agreed.

Fisk figured that having a female attorney representing Richards, especially one who was savvy, battle-tested, hard-minded, and able to go the distance, would help the case, should it ever make it to court—not that he intended for the case ever to go to court. Just as doctors make lousy patients, lawyers make lousy clients. True to form, Richards would turn out to be the worst client Denise had ever encountered.

Her first encounter with Daniel Richards happened when he strode into her office unannounced, accompanied by one of his junior associates. Denise recognized Richards, and nodded to Lisa, who trailed helplessly in his wake, unable to forewarn her boss, that it was okay.

Richards introduced himself with a brief handshake that was excessively firm and left Denise's hand tingling. The dark eyes that looked directly into hers were flat and cold, like a shark's. It was apparent that Richards would be calling all the shots, and she would merely perform according to script.

Normally, in divorce cases where infidelity was a factor, Denise explained, one of the first items was the hiring of a private detective. However, this was not a normal case, and Daniel Richards was not an average client. He was already fully prepared. Even more savvy, battle-tested, hard-minded, and ready to do combat with a meat axe than Denise, he had already taken the liberty of hiring his own detective. As he explained, the utmost discretion had been needed, and all the necessary investigation had been taken care of. His assistant laid a neatly bound folder on her desk.

"Here you will find everything that is needed to settle this case," Richards said.

Looking through it, Denise found it contained several reports from one of the most expensive detective agencies in the city, along with numerous photographs of the current Mrs. Richards, many of them showing her and a companion in compromisingly intimate situations. Denise had seen reports and photos from private eyes before, but even she found these remarkably graphic. Indeed, the folder contained all that was needed to settle—but the price shocked even her.

"This is rather extreme, Mr. Richards," she said, closing the folder. "Are you sure you want to go this far?"

"Yes, this is exactly what I want," Richards said bluntly. "If you're squeamish, well . . ."

"I'm not squeamish, sir," she countered. "But it is my responsibility to point out the repercussions that may ensue, particularly if in time you decide not to proceed with the divorce."

"Reconciliation with my dear wife is not an option at this point," he said. "The marriage is over, and I want the matter settled once and for all—and quickly."

He stood, indicating the meeting was over. The assistant closed his briefcase with a crisp snap and also stood, taking a place slightly to the side and just behind his employer. As Richards moved, so did the assistant, as though they were performing a well-rehearsed shadow dance.

Daniel Richards again shook Denise's hand as he made his farewell, but this time he didn't release his grip. "I trust that you will be capable of handling this . . . matter appropriately, Ms. Ryland?"

"Yes, sir, you can count on me," she answered. Nodding approval, Richards exerted a bit more pressure on her hand before he released it and gave her a tight-lipped smile, a cold one that didn't reach his eyes. He glided out of her office, the assistant trailing close behind, as abruptly as he arrived. Denise watched him, rubbing her hand and suppressing a shiver.

Richards' investigation of his wife had been thorough. It bordered on being illegal, but when one rode as high as Daniel Richards did, that was a mere technicality to be ignored. Linda Richards had indeed been having an affair—in fact, since the ink had dried on the marriage license, she'd had more than one. Deception and subterfuge were apparently not new to her, and she had been unusually clever in covering her tracks. Unfortunately for her, like most cheating spouses, she had overlooked a few things, and it was no problem for an experienced and expert hunter like her husband to pick up the trail and bring her to bay.

Daniel Richards had hired not one, but two of the detective agency's Sherlocks to follow his wife. From the amount of information in the folder given to Denise, Linda Richards had been under observation almost from day one.

In the folder Richards left with Denise were time and date records of his wife's comings and goings, transcripts of telephone conversations, and photographs and a dozen hours of videotaped encounters randy enough to make a porn queen blush. Denise shook her head in wonder; from what Richards had spent on surveillance, the private dicks he'd hired could probably now buy lakeshore homes in Evanston.

Richards had the tenacity of a rottweiler, and it was reflected in the strategy he'd outlined for Denise. The case was to be settled out of court. And he was not about to pay the exorbitant amount his wife was demanding. Period. Richards was counting on what few scruples his wife had, and the fact that she had been with her current lover for eight months—a record for her—and this time was head over heels in love. The problem: her paramour was a married man with three children. She could accept the proposed settlement, or a copy of the report would be delivered not only to the man's wife, but also his employer, thus ruining his life and destroying whatever chance they had to be together. The fact that the lives of the man's family would also be destroyed was of no consequence to Richards.

Normally, these things would be of little or no consequence to Denise, either, but even she was struck by the viciousness Richards demonstrated. It became apparent that marriage meant little to him, a mere formality, and fidelity within marriage mattered even less. More than likely, he'd also had at least one affair in the past couple of years, but he had the resources to ensure that no trace could be detected. Nor did the money really matter; Richards had the kind of wealth that seemed limitless. What did matter to Daniel Richards was his pride. His wife hadn't had the good sense to be truly discreet, and word of her dalliances had gotten around.

Perhaps it was somewhat his own fault. Richards had met his wife during a period when he was uncharacteristically vulnerable. Spotting her at a banquet as she served cocktails, he was attracted by her long golden hair, green eyes, and youthful appearance. She was working her way though college toward her latest career endeavor as an interior decorator, which he found charming. Thinking she would be a pleasant diversion for the weekend, he flirted and she responded.

After a couple of weekends, though, he became enchanted by her. Despite the fact that she was not quite as youthful as her appearance first led him to believe, she nonetheless demonstrated many enticing qualities, some of which even he was amazed that a person's body was capable of doing. He found her crudeness a challenge, and began to think of her as a gem in the rough, one that could be refined, cut, and polished, and once in the proper setting, would be a valuable jewel, and that flattered his image of himself.

Daniel Richards was getting much more than he had bargained for, though. Anyone who really knew Linda knew how crafty she could be. With a reputation as a hard-boiled but hot hootchie-mama, she picked her settings carefully, going from job to job at only the very best establishments, searching and waiting for the perfect husband material to come along. Not just anyone, though; the perfect candidate had to be a Mercedes-driving, lunch-at-the-country-club, Gold Coast apartment, fifty-four-foot cabin cruiser, weekends in Vail, European vacation kind of guy. She was attracted to the power that was associated with Richards' type of high-class, big-shot lawyer, just as he was to her bosomy size-six figure. She thought that he was wonderful—an opinion he shared.

Linda quickly adapted to dining in five-star restaurants and staying in five-star hotels, wearing silver fox and sable, kicking around in designer originals, jetting to Paris and Rome for shopping sprees, and filling her medicine cabinets at Richards' apartment with the finest cosmetics. It was a lifestyle she had dreamed of having for so long, and she became addicted to it.

Unfortunately, as marital discord mounted and the romantic dream died, Linda Richards faced a new dilemma. Panicked, she realized that without her husband, she would be excluded from the world of the Bentley and Tiffany's crowd. Determined to hold onto her affluent lifestyle, she prowled for and found a new suitor.

Since one attorney had gotten her where she wanted to be, she figured if she found another attorney, she had a chance of standing pat. Finally, she found what she was looking for. On the downside, though, her new beau was married. However, because his wife wasn't much of a socializer, preferring to stay home with the kiddies, it was easy for Linda to step into a vacant slot in his life.

It dawned on Denise that the real reason for Daniel Richards' fury wasn't so much that his ex-wife was involved with another man, or that she had been less than impeccably discreet. It was that she was involved with another attorney—a member of the "club." In a profession where everyone knew everyone else, for a man as high-powered as Daniel Richards to be cuckolded by one of his own, and an inferior at that, was humiliating beyond description. Denise knew from her rural upbringing that nothing was more dangerous than a wounded animal, and Daniel Richards would gnaw his own leg off to escape from the trap he was in, destroying anyone who got in his way.

Denise had no problem helping Richards get what he wanted. What did complicate things was that the "other man" was Jacob Hamilton. Not only had Denise gone to law school with Hamilton, he was also a good friend, and she and Jerry frequently socialized with Jake and his wife. Denise knew that the Hamiltons' marriage had been rocky for several years now, but he loved his children and Denise had assumed that he and his wife would ultimately work things out. His involvement with Linda Richards could very well put the kibosh on everything.

Denise was tempted to call her friend and let him know what he was in store for, but from an ethical standpoint, she couldn't. Attorney-client confidentiality was sacred, and if she breached that, her career could be seriously damaged, if not ruined. She had to put her client first—but wasn't this client different? The more she thought about Daniel Richards, the more revolting she found him. To her, his single-minded quest for vengeance and disregard for fairness and the consequences to others made him, in Denise's eyes, the kind of lawyer who gave attorneys a bad name.

No one was more driven to win cases than Denise. Her fierce determination was an integral part of her success, but she had never acted with malicious intent. Daniel Richards was bent on destruction and Denise wouldn't allow that to happen to a colleague and his family, people she truly cared about.

Denise had never let personal feelings interfere with business, and she didn't want to let them do so now. Setting the folder from the private eyes aside, she busied herself organizing the notes she'd taken during the meeting with Richards and going over the settlement specifications his assistant had left with her. As she had been instructed, she dictated the settlement offer Daniel Richards was making to his wife and had Lisa type it up right away.

She sat brooding as she contemplated the dilemma facing her. Her ability to compartmentalize was one of her strong points and an integral part of her success, and she was reluctant to veer from that now, but she thought Daniel Richards was about as down and dirty as a person could be. Furthermore, she knew Jacob Hamilton was basically a decent guy, and even though he had made a mistake—in this case, a big one—he didn't deserve to be destroyed. She looked through her Rolodex for Hamilton's number and called and asked him to meet her for lunch.

She was sitting at a corner table at the Caribou Lounge brooding over an apricot iced tea when Jake Hamilton arrived. They exchanged greetings and pleasantries. He asked about Jerry and she inquired about Estelle and the boys, and admired the photos of his family which he proudly showed her.

"We've been meaning to have you and Jerry over to grill some swordfish, but something always seems to come up," Jake said.

"I know how that goes," Denise answered. "We've been pretty busy too."

The waiter appeared and described the lunch specials, and Denise and Jake placed their orders. The waiter left, and Denise became somber.

"Jake, how are things going with you and Estelle?" she asked.

He flushed and fiddled with his water glass, stabbing at the slice of lemon in it with his straw. "We're okay, I guess. You know how it is when you've been married for a long time."

He looked her squarely in the eye. "What's this all about, Denise?" he asked. "I know something's up or you wouldn't have called out of the blue and wanted to meet for lunch."

"I've been hired to represent someone in a divorce, and I won't mention any names, but this situation is about as rotten as a person wanting to destroy another person can get . . ." She hesitated. "My client commissioned these 'works of art,' and they're going to fry your eyeballs." She handed an envelope to him. "Jake, please understand—I'm showing you these as a friend, not as an attorney."

He took the envelope and opened it. He slid the contents out and as he looked over them, the blood drained from his face. There were pictures of him and Linda together in various situations, everything from opening-night galas to intimate dinners to passionate encounters in fancy hotel rooms. He was amazed at the large volume of information before him and mortified at the thought of what he had done. He knew these pictures would fall like an atom bomb on a marriage that still had a lot of good things in it—not to mention his career.

"And I've got twelve of these," Denise added, holding up a videotape cassette.

He was unable to look at Denise. "I can only imagine what you must think of me," he said.

"What I think of you—or about this—doesn't matter, but I want to help you, so you have to help me, and we have to move fast. We both know what this particular husband is capable of," Denise said. "First of all, is it over between you and Linda Richards?" He nodded miserably.

"That much is good," she said. "But there's another, bigger problem." Jake looked at her quizzically. "Somehow, you've got to get Linda to accept this settlement offer or these"—she gestured toward the envelope of photos—"are likely to be marked as evidence and used in court against her. And you know Richards will leak them to Estelle, your employer, and the media—and they'll have a field day with it."

They paused when the waiter brought their meals. They each took a few bites, but in their present state of mind, the food tasted like cardboard, and they shoved the plates aside.

Denise reached over and placed her hand compassionately on Jake's. "Will Linda talk to you?" she asked.

"I don't know. She might."

"We don't have much time," Denise persisted.

"I'll call her right away," he said, standing. "Don't worry, I'll take care of it somehow."

Denise watched him as he left the restaurant stepped onto the sidewalk. He fished his cell phone out of his pocket and punched in a number, and she suspected that he was calling Linda Richards. He spoke rapidly, punctuating his conversation with a few wild gestures, then snapped the phone shut and hailed a taxi.

When Jake arrived at Linda's apartment, he told her about the settlement offer. Just as Denise had predicted, Linda went totally berserk. She had always known her husband was ruthless and played foul hardball, but she never expected him to aim at her. She refused to even consider the offer until Jacob handed her the photos that Denise had given him. She was astounded. Who had secured this information? How did they do it? Some low-life had dogged her every step from her aerobics classes to the stall in the ladies' room.

Her own future was bombed, but she didn't want to drag Jacob down with her. Linda realized that she couldn't do anything but accept the offer under the circumstances. She looked the paper over again. In crisp legal terms, the document outlined how, because Linda Richards had flagrantly abused her husband's trust and voided their prenuptial agreement with her tactless infidelities, the amount of settlement upon divorce would be drastically reduced. The settlement offer was for one dollar. It was worse than getting nothing—it was insulting. Daniel Richards obviously intended to knock her to the pavement and steamroller her into oblivion. Despondent, she realized also that she would now have to go back to serving beer and sweeping peanuts off a barroom floor in order to finish college.

Jacob Hamilton was desperate. He sympathized with her and himself ranted over the unfairness of the settlement, but he didn't see how she could avoid signing it. Knowing that he had so much more to lose than the money she was so upset over, he mustered all the skills he'd fine-tuned in the courtroom over the years and worked to convince her.

"You're angry, and you have every right to be," he said. "And I don't want to see you left high and dry. I will help you out if you sign."

They worked out an agreement where he would finance the rest of her education, and although he didn't have the resources to make up for her prenup settlement of two hundred thousand dollars, he would at least pay her rent and, when he could, introduce her to eligible men in the right circles.

Grumbling, she signed the agreement. There were two copies; she kept one, and Jake took the other. Then with promises to be in touch soon, he left her to her dark thoughts.

Linda picked up the envelope that held the photos and with a howl of rage, hurled it across the room. When it landed, a business card fluttered out. She bent over and picked the card up. Printed on it was DENISE RYLAND, ATTORNEY AT LAW, along with Denise's phone number, fax number, and e-mail address. So that was the designing woman who had put the dirty little package together. Linda picked up the phone and furiously punched in the number.

Lisa, Denise's secretary, answered. Linda explained who she was, and Lisa transferred the call to Denise. When Denise answered the phone, she was shocked at the venom in the caller's voice.

"I hope you're happy, you bitch," Linda began. "One dollar—one stinking dollar! I deserve what I had coming in that prenup!" She drew a ragged breath and continued her tirade. "You think you're so smart, and Jake thinks you're such a little goody-goody. He told me how you and your husband vacationed with him and Estelle in Europe last year and that you're godparents to his boys. But I know what you really are."

Denise tried to get a word in. "Mrs. Richards, I really don't think this is appropriate—"

Linda ignored her. "What you're doing to me is about as low as you can get—having me followed like a common criminal! How the hell do you sleep at night, knowing the garbage you throw at people ruins their lives?"

"Now, just hold on. I had nothing to do—" Denise tried to say before being interrupted again.

"Oh, just save it!" Linda Richards snarled. "Everyone knows about your dirty underhanded tactics. I know all about your little detective—Romanowski, Ranski, or whatever the hell his name is. Jake once told me all about him, how you pay him to sneak around at midnight peeking into people's bedrooms. He's probably the one you hired to follow me. Bad enough you did it to me, another woman—you don't even know me—but you did it to your so-called friend Jake! Just remember, what goes around comes around. One of these days you'll get yours, you miserable, stinking bitch!"

Linda slammed the phone down and it took Denise a moment before it sank in that the connection had been broken. She was incredulous at Linda Richards' savage verbal attack. After all, it wasn't she who had hired the detective who collected the information, nor had she had anything to do with the ridiculous settlement offer. However, it was her name on all the paperwork and all the files, so, of course, Linda blamed her for the whole mess. There was no doubt in Denise's mind that Jake probably held her partially responsible as well. The insidiousness of Daniel Richards' manipulations was going to sully her own life as well.

Not that Daniel Richards cared at all. He had won, and that was all that mattered. The case was settled on his terms, and rumor had it that he was in panting pursuit of wife number four. Denise had done his dirty work and he had boldly moved on to his next conquest. Aggravated, Denise decided that she would make sure to bill him extra for that convenience.

7

May 1998
Case Number FR007218

"After a long dry spell it looks as if we're finally going to get some rainfall. If your lawn is as brown as mine, then you know we really need the moisture. A developing storm system over the Great Plains will send a wave of strong thunderstorms our way. While the spring rains will be welcome, we'll have to watch out for the possibility of severe weather tomorrow afternoon. The good news is that after almost two years of below normal precip, up to two inches of rain is likely over the next twenty-four hours."

—NBC 5 Chicago meteorologist Brant Miller

Over the years, Denise had learned the value of background information. To her, the difference between a good attorney and a not-so-good one was the amount of information in hand when the trial or the settlement drew near.

It was not important how the information was obtained or how much the information cost. The cost could always be passed on to the client. The only things that mattered were that the information was reliable and that it was damaging. For most people, there was usually some kind of family secret, scandal, or skeleton tucked back in the dark closet among the shoes, shirts, and dirty laundry. The right person could figure where and how to dig deep enough to exhume the bones.

Denise Ryland knew of such an earthmover. Linda Richards had taken his name in vain, but she had him pegged right.

Dale Romanski was a former Chicago PD detective. He and Denise had met by chance years ago in the justice center commissary during a divorce case.

Denise's client in that particular case had been a discarded wife. The sweetheart of Sigma Chi had been traded in for a hot-wired new love and was about to lose everything that she valued in the process. Her husband was a local insurance agent; she had been a founding partner in their small but successful agency specializing in insuring drivers with poor driving records.

For almost thirty years, the wife and husband had worked side by side to build a successful business, slaving late into the evening tabulating invoices and processing applications for coverage, taking time only to run out for burgers or pizza, eaten at their desks, and then dropping into bed after eighteen-hour days. The agency was now worth over twenty million dollars and the husband wanted it all. He insisted that his wife had been no more than "a glorified secretary," merely helping him, the true brains of the organization. As his logic ran, he had given her three children, now grown, a roof over her head, and the clothes on her back. Thus, she had already been well-compensated through the years, and had no further claims against the business.

His settlement offer was an insulting three hundred thousand dollars, with no alimony. In those long-ago days, Denise didn't know how she was going to prove the full value of her client's contributions over the years. She had not been with the firm long, but she knew she needed to win this case to show that she could come through even when she had little evidence to substantiate her case.

Detective Sergeant Dale Romanski happened to be at the courthouse late one Friday morning, killing time until he was to testify in a case slated during the afternoon session. He loved hanging out in courtrooms, relishing the tense atmosphere and watching the wheels of the legal system turn.

As he observed the divorce case in progress, he was impressed with the young African-American attorney with the honeyed Southern accent who represented the wife. He soon realized the young woman's soft, gentle accent was deceptive, and her strong courtroom demeanor, matching her feisty temperament, reminded him of his daughter. In fact, Denise and his daughter would have been about the same age—had Angela lived.

During a recess, he spotted Denise in the justice center commissary having lunch with her client. He introduced himself, and pulled up a chair and sat at their table. They made small talk until the client left, and then he told Denise he had observed enough to know her case was in trouble, and that he also had some information that he thought could help her. In a totally unrelated investigation, he said, he had learned that the owner of a local insurance agency had been photographed in the company of some women who worked for a local "escort" service. The name of Denise's client had rung a bell, and he'd done a little checking. Coincidentally, the man in the pictures in question was the estranged husband of Denise's client.

At Romanski's suggestion, Denise requested a recess for the weekend in order to assess the information. At first she didn't know what to think of the detective. He wasn't much taller than she, slightly built, and seemingly very laid-back in attitude. But appearances were often deceiving, she knew, and she sensed that behind his calm facade was a steely reserve. Looking into his eyes, she was sure her assumption was correct. Also, it was clear that Romanski knew what he was talking about, and since she could see no other way to save her case, she took his advice and they met the next day.

At the meeting, he handed her an envelope that contained some very revealing pictures of her client's husband. Denise was stunned.

"Why are you being so generous?" she asked him. "After all, we don't even know each other. What's in this for you?"

"Hey, not everyone's gotta have an angle," he responded dryly. "Us legal types, we gotta fly together. Besides, kid, somebody's gotta pull your fat out of the fire. Why not me?"

When court resumed on Monday, Denise conferred with her opposing counsel and informed him of the new information in her possession. The insurance agent, when his attorney described the situation to him, was overwhelmed with an uncharacteristic wave of generosity. Armed with the pictures Romanski gave her, Denise was able to win her client a ten-million-dollar settlement, eight thousand dollars a month in spousal support, the house, the Lexus, the yacht club membership, and the accompanying yacht. Denise walked away with a sizable fee and a healthy bonus from her appreciative employer.

Denise also came out of the case having gained a new colleague and friend, someone she knew she could always depend on. Romanski never let her down; over the years the two of them often shared lunch in the justice center commissary or dined on Mexican or Chinese food in nearby neighborhood haunts. They became steadfast friends.

Of Polish descent, Romanski was a native Chicagoan. He was a quiet man who listened more than he spoke. A drunk driver had killed his wife and teenage daughter in a car accident fifteen years before, and he had never remarried. While he and Denise were different in many ways, they found that they shared many things in common. They both felt a passionate hatred of Chicago's winters filled with lake-effect snow and sub-zero temperatures, and a deep love of the legal system and its inner workings.

After twenty-one years as an underpaid public servant, Romanski decided to go into the private sector. Denise was his first client, and over time she made sure that she frequently slid business his way. He was a methodical investigator with extensive contacts in the various police departments in the Chicago area, and could always be counted on to sift through dim passageways and trash-filled back alleys to find the information she needed.

Nine months had passed since the Grandma Murders trial had ended. Jimmy George Hinson, as many had expected, had been given the ultimate penalty and was a resident on death row in Joliet. His sister LaVergne had finally quit writing outraged letters to Denise.

As a partner, Denise was given only high-profile cases, and the one that faced her in the fresh spring air of May 1998 was unusually prickly. Clive Phillips, director of the Newville High School Performing Panthers marching band and drill team, was accused of battery, statutory rape, child abuse, child endangerment, criminal confinement, and rape in an assault on a fourteen-year-old girl, a flutist in the band. In addition to the criminal charges against the teacher, the girl's parents were suing the school and the school board for over two million dollars.

Denise was representing the Newville School Board. Mr. Phillips, a teacher for twenty-two years at Newville High School, had a spotless record, at least until now. Under his direction, the Performing Panthers had strutted and twirled their way to fourteen first-place awards in the Illinois State marching band competition. In the school lobby, the trophy case was filled with shiny cups and plaques his groups had earned over the years at the State Fair. They had traveled to a presidential inauguration and to the Rose Bowl, impressing parade route spectators every step of the way. Now their director was in the worst kind of trouble in which a teacher could find himself.

As was her usual practice, Denise called on her private snoop. She filled Romanski in on the details on the lawsuit. From the information she had, it looked like an open and shut case, with Clive Phillips definitely guilty of the charges. She needed something to turn any and all responsibility away from the school and the school board, and get the lawsuit dropped. Perhaps there was something in the girl's background . . .

"Check out the whole family, Dale," she said to Romanski. "My back's against the wall, and I need something good."

Romanski assured her he'd look into it carefully, and get back with her in a few days. Confident that he would deliver what she needed, she hung up the phone and smiled.

8

A week later Denise received Dale Romanski's report. The rape victim's mother, Jeanine Boatman, was a native Chicagoan who had lived several years in Wisconsin after being orphaned as a child. She was a registered nurse employed at Chicago General Hospital. Her background was otherwised unremarkable except for an emotional breakdown after her divorce from her first husband, requiring a brief hospitalization. The woman had no criminal record and her work record was exemplary. She was not close to any of her coworkers, and none of them had ever been to her home or actually met her husband or daughter. She was civil and cordial with her neighbors, but not actually friends with any of them either. In fact, the woman seemed to have no close friends.

Denise scanned over the report on the victim herself and couldn't find anything there either. A freshman at school, Cheryl was an honor student with plans to attend Northwestern. She played the flute with the school band, was an honor-roll student, and never had been in any kind of trouble. Cheryl Boatman was, as Denise's mama would say, as white as wool. The girl had no boyfriends, didn't date at all.

Damn, Denise thought. This would not do at all. There had to be some way to discredit this girl or her family. What was needed was dirt—deep dirt.

Denise turned to Romanski's report on girl's stepfather, Tucker Boatman. At last, something that could help Hurricane Denise blow this suit out of the water.

According to the report, Boatman was a real piece of work. He had married Cheryl's mother when Cheryl was three and adopted the little girl. Life was no bed of roses for the family, though, and more often than not, Boatman remained unemployed. Currently he was working as a supervisor for a janitorial service. His background included a laundry list of minor scrapes with the law that had landed him in and out of jail several times. He had also served a two-year stint at Joliet on a burglary charge.

All that was small potatoes, and not enough to even consider. One item, though, caught Denise's full attention. Five years ago, during a sleepover for Cheryl's ninth birthday, Tucker Boatman had been found in a somewhat compromising position with an eight-year-old girl.

The nine little girls attending the party had, as expected, snacked on pizza, pop, and birthday cake. With that kind of carbo high, they had chattered and giggled until late into the night, after which they had crawled into their sleeping bags scattered all over the living room in the small three-bedroom, one-bathroom ranch home and crashed. The house finally quiet, Jeanine and Tucker Boatman, who had gone to bed earlier, finally were able to go to sleep.

A couple of hours later nature called, and Tucker, still half asleep, headed to the bathroom. Not wanting to wake himself up, he didn't bother to turn on the bathroom light; he also forgot to shut the door. He had just finished his business and was ready to head back to bed when the light came on. He turned and there stood Marcie Taylor, one of the little girls at the sleepover. Unfortunately, Tucker's PJ's tended to gap and the child, seeing more of a grown man than any kid would ever want to see, responded as most grossed-out little girls would do: she screamed.

Tucker, still groggy and confused by the situation, attempted to calm and hopefully quiet the girl. He grabbed her by the shoulders and with one hand covered her mouth, shushing her and trying to reassure her that everything was okay. Marcie continued to squirm and try to wriggle out of his grasp, but his grip was firm. He almost had her calmed down when he heard a noise at the bathroom door; there stood young Cheryl and the other children, with his wife pushing through the group, demanding to know what was going on.

Tucker explained, and Marcie more or less corroborated his story. Things settled down and everyone went back to bed. The next morning, amid the Lucky Charms, Cocoa Puffs, and orange juice, none of the kids said anything about the night's incident, and everything seemed okay. They packed up their sleeping bags and jammies and headed home, and the Boatmans returned to life as usual.

Or so they thought. They had not counted on how much eight- and nine-year-old girls love to talk. One child told her mother about Marcie and Mr. Boatman; that mother then called other mothers, who then got the story from their daughters. Of course, each child had a somewhat different version, and with all the interest their parents were showing, some of the girls added a few embellishments. Marcie's parents, naturally, were beside themselves. As a result, what had been nothing more than an innocent although embarrassing bump-in-the-night incident, through gossip and misinterpretation, turned into a full-scale perverted tale of attempted child molestation.

Parents all over town were enraged and the police were called. Tucker Boatman explained what had happened, and upon questioning, Marcie Taylor also told the truth, and nothing but. Nevertheless, the damage had been done, and with his prior criminal record, the townspeople's minds were made up.

Pending further investigation, Tucker Boatman was arrested on preliminary charges of indecent exposure, child molestation, and assault. The cops wanted to be sure that the little girl in question had not been under any kind of duress when she said Boatman had done nothing to her. After two days, the child's family didn't want to press charges, and since there was nothing concrete to hold him on, he was released.

Feeling terrible about the whole thing, Tucker went to the Taylor home to try to apologize for the misunderstanding and to be sure the child was all right. Unfortunately, Marcie now thought he was too icky for words and refused to even see him. He persisted, and the Taylors threatened to call the police if he didn't leave at once. They obtained a restraining order, and by now the incident had caught the attention of the Chicago Department of Child and Family Services, who proceeded to conduct a thorough investigation. Their findings were inconclusive. Tucker was cleared of all wrongdoing and the charges were dropped.

It was too late, though. Tucker Boatman had become a pariah in the community, and negative sentiment toward him lingered. Regardless of the outcome of the investigation, in the eyes of his neighbors, he was guilty. His supposed guilt was unfairly transferred onto his wife and daughter; local merchants made shopping almost impossible, and none of the neighborhood children were allowed to play with Cheryl anymore. There was nothing left to do but move and hope the dark cloud didn't follow them.

Thus, the Boatman family packed up and moved to suburban Newville. Things went well, and word of the horrible debacle did not follow. They began life anew; Jeanine no longer kept all the curtains drawn, and Cheryl did well in school and made lots of new friends. At last they could put the whole ugly mess behind them, and things returned to normal—except that Tucker Boatman never again went to the bathroom at home without turning on the light and shutting and locking the door.

Denise Ryland closed the cover on the report and smiled. This information was going to make her job a whole lot easier. It was obvious that the last thing the Boatmans wanted was for that nasty episode to rear itself again and ruin the life they had now. Getting them to drop the lawsuit would be a piece of cake. Denise made mental note that Dale Romanski would get a bonus for this.

To justify her plan, Denise told herself that in spite of the fact that Clive Phillips had made a huge mistake, he was a decent man and didn't deserve to go to prison and have his career destroyed. Granted, Cheryl Boatman was an innocent victim of tragic circumstance, but she was young and would get over it. She had her whole life ahead of her. No big deal.

9

When Denise examined the full story of the rape case, she realized it was indeed a big deal. What she discovered affected the way she would construct the school board case. She would need to use all her skill and cunning, because Clive Phillips had indeed behaved very badly.

Cheryl Boatman was a young girl who had grown old in one short night. After moving to Newville, the Boatman family had successfully put the past behind them. Cheryl had fit in well in the new neighborhood and become one of the most popular girls in the community. She made good grades in school and was a reliable and much-sought-after baby-sitter. She also was a talented musician who played the flute like an angel and participated in the band in junior high. Naturally, she'd auditioned for both the orchestra and band in high school and was promptly accepted.

In his two decades as a high school band director, Clive Phillips was always on the lookout for students with potential. With his assistance, many young people were able to attend summer band camps, and several students had won music scholarships so that they would continue to study in college and perhaps find a career in music. Phillips loved music with every fiber of his being, and he loved working with young people as much. A life-long bachelor, it was often joked around the town that he was married to his work.

Cheryl Boatman's talent caught Phillips' interest right away. Not only did she have a natural ear for music, but she was a good sight-reader as well. Even though she was only a freshman, she was one of the best flutists Phillips had ever taught. With the proper care and attention, he was certain Cheryl would be a star, blazing her way to the success and fame he had always dreamed of for himself, but knew he would never achieve.

One day after rehearsal, he asked Cheryl if she would care to take private lessons. There would be no charge, he reassured her when she began to protest, and besides, if she practiced and learned enough to sufficiently develop her skills, she most likely would earn a scholarship to any school of her choice, even Julliard. He could schedule the lessons right there at school, he said, and they could meet before first period for one hour, two days per week. Flattered by the attention, she agreed and the sessions began.

Cheryl was indeed a model protégé, and she flourished under the extra attention. After a month, Phillips expanded the sessions to three days a week. Cheryl's sight-reading improved quickly, and by the second semester she moved to first chair in the orchestra. Phillips was overjoyed with his find, and as the time for the spring concert approached, he added to the repertoire some new music designed to showcase his star pupil.

The spring concert was the highlight of the school year for the music program. It was the largest fund-raiser of the year. A number of Mr. Phillips' former students had come for the festivities; two of them played for the Chicago Philharmonic and one for the Dallas Symphony.

For Clive Phillips, this was the biggest night of the year, made even better because of his new prodigy. The auditorium was filled to capacity; in fact, it seemed as if the whole town of Newville had turned out to indulge in the sumptuous musical feast.

The concert began, filling the spring night with classic favorites ranging from pieces of Gershwin's *Rhapsody in Blue* to an excerpt of Tchaikowski's *1812 Overture*. The audience eagerly anticipated their favorite feature of the spring concert, an original composition penned by their very own Clive Phillips, always a splendid finale to the program.

This year he had created a lovely and ornate sonatina featuring a flute solo. He had written it especially for Cheryl, designed it to display her mastery and talent.

He introduced the piece, then held his breath as Cheryl played. The notes bubbled from her flute, and she handled the most difficult parts of the composition with seemingly little effort. The many mornings of practice had paid off. Clive Phillips' face glowed with pride and satisfaction. Truly, truly, his pupil's poise and ability were a reflection of her teacher's success.

The music ended and the ovation was thunderous. Cheryl's eyes glowed and her smile lit up the auditorium. Her proud parents dabbed tears from their eyes as Clive Phillips presented a bouquet of roses to his young pupil. It was the most glorious night of both his and the girl's life.

As the orchestra filed backstage to put their instruments away, Phillips, always the conscientious educator, took pains to praise each of the young musicians. The annual spring concert was the orchestra's biggest event, and they all had worked hard. Surely, life could not possibly be better than it was at that moment for Clive Phillips. All of his hard work with these young musicians, all of the coddling, coaxing, and encouragement, the fumbling fingers that, under his guidance, had at last become supple and skilled—it had all been worth it. And the crowning glory was to have such a gem as young Cheryl. As the youngsters milled about, preparing to go off to the post-concert gala, Phillips' eyes glistened and his heart swelled with pride.

However, he was about to hit a very sour note. "Pride goeth before a fall," Denise Ryland's mama would have said. And so it was to be.

10

What happened later was a grim drama set against an incongruously festive background.

A long-time tradition was the Musicians' Ball that was held afterward in the school gymnasium to honor the young musicians. Several couples attending, many of them alumni, reminisced how their budding romances had blossomed at the ball in years past, and as beads of light sparkled off a spinning crystal ball, sweethearts of all ages swayed together as the school's jazz band played soft music. A still beaming Cheryl stood near the door, surveying the scene. Clive Phillips, accompanied by a young man, approached her and handed her a cup of punch.

"Your performance tonight was outstanding, Cheryl," he said. "You played even better than I thought you would."

"Oh, thank you, Mr. Phillips," Cheryl replied. "I was so nervous, but I kept remembering what you said, to just concentrate on the music and forget about the audience."

Phillips introduced her to his companion. Robert Anton was a former student who now was a cellist with the Dallas Symphony. He always tried to come home for the spring concert, Phillips explained.

Anton expressed his appreciation of her performance. "Cheryl, your artistry truly is remarkable for one so young," he said. "It's obvious that you have a gift. I wouldn't be a bit surprised to find myself accompanying *you* some day."

Cheryl thanked him, blushing. "Mr. Phillips wrote the music. I just played it."

"And play it you did, my dear. It was as if it poured from your heart," Phillips said, beaming like a proud parent.

It seemed that everyone was proud of her and, for the first time in her life, Cheryl was truly proud of herself. This night was the stuff of dreams, and she was a fairy princess, the center of admiration and adoration. It was all sparkle and glitter, and all totally unreal.

The ball continued, and a light rain began to fall, misting the large windows that lined both sides of the old un-air-conditioned gymnasium; it was nothing major at first, just a gentle sprinkling that cooled the warm spring air. Nothing could dampen the festive mood in the gymnasium, though. Parents, teachers, and students mingled and danced. Still glowing with pride over their daughter, Jeanine and Tucker Boatman sipped punch and happily accepted the glowing remarks from other parents and teachers. Usually uncomfortable in social situations such as this one, even Tucker seemed to be enjoying himself.

Cheryl waved to her parents as she waltzed by in the arms of Chuck Malinsky, a sophomore who played drums with the orchestra. The music ended, and she and Chuck walked over to the bleachers and sat down.

Cheryl had decided to wear a pair of shoes with a chunky, three-inch heel and a one-inch platform sole. They were the coolest shoes she'd ever owned, and she loved the way she looked in them, but, boy, did they hurt. She looked at the clock on the gym wall. It was only eight o'clock. The ball was scheduled to last until ten, but she knew her feet wouldn't, not in these shoes. She had another pair of shoes in the bag she'd stashed in the auditorium with her flute case, in a storeroom backstage. They were just a pair of flats, but they had to feel better than the shoes she had on now. Grudgingly, she decided to switch, and she limped out of the gym toward the storeroom, calling to her parents that she'd be right back.

Cheryl opened the door to the storeroom and felt for the light switch. Unable to find it, she decided the light from the hallway would suffice. She found the bag with her other shoes, and slipped the platforms off. Suddenly, a shadow blocked the light and she whirled, startled.

"Oh, Mr. Phillips!" she gasped. "You scared me half to death!"

"I'm sorry, Cheryl," he said. "But I saw you leave the gym, and I . . . I thought . . ." He blinked and looked confused, as if he were unsure exactly *what* he was thinking. He stepped inside the storeroom.

Cheryl took a step backward, the hair prickling the back of her neck. He was looking at her so strangely, it made her uneasy. She was being silly, she told herself; it's just Mr. Phillips. Still . . .

"Is . . . is there something you wanted to tell me?" she asked, trying to move around him toward the door. The storeroom suddenly felt so small.

"Yes, Cheryl, there is something I want to say." He cleared his throat. "I want to say that you are . . . you were, that is . . ." Dear Lord, what was he doing? He gazed at her; she was so lovely.

"You are so talented, so beautiful, and tonight you are stunning," he blurted, and pulled her to him and kissed her on the cheek. Alarmed by his behavior, she pulled away and tried to slip past him and out of the storeroom.

"Mr. Phillips, I have to go—"

He grabbed her arm and pushed the door shut.

"Mr. Phillips, don't! What are you doing?" she truly was frightened now and struggled to escape his grasp. In the dim light that filtered in from the crack around the door, his wild-eyed and disheveled appearance alarmed her.

He shook his head in bewilderment. "Please forgive me, Cheryl," he said. "I guess I just lost my head."

He was mortified. He had been an educator for twenty years and had never had a problem maintaining the proper teacher-student relationship. Yet here before him, instead of an innocent teenaged schoolgirl, he saw only the epitome of the perfect woman, a Circe for whom he lusted.

"It's okay, Mr. Phillips, just don't do it again," she said nervously. When he didn't move, she inched toward the door again. "Look, Mr. Phillips, I really do have to go now."

He still didn't move. After a few seconds of awkward silence, he spoke.

"It was the kiss. I meant nothing by it, but maybe I went too far. I meant no disrespect, Cheryl, you have to believe me. It's just that you played so well, and you look so sweet." He paused and then seemed to lose all restraint. "You see, my dear, you've been special from the beginning. Your talent, your enthusiasm . . . You are a joy to me—I adore you."

He started to speak again but she held up her hand, palm facing him, to silence him. "It's okay, really," she said.

He held out his hand to her. "Are we still friends? Shake?"

Cheryl bit her lip. Maybe if she shook hands with him he would let her go. He was really creeping her out now, and she just wanted to get out of the tiny storeroom, find her parents, and go home. Tentatively, she reached out and took his hand. "Okay, friends," she said.

She started to pull her hand away, but he held onto it and, raising it to his lips, kissed her fingers. As thunder rumbled in the distance, she jerked her hand away but he grabbed her by the shoulders and pulled her to him.

"I know this is wrong but . . . oh, God, I love you—I so desperately want to be with you." He gazed deep into her eyes. Time seemed to stand still.

"I'm sorry—you can't—" She frantically searched the darkened room, looking for another escape route. The storeroom was remote; the door closed. Should she scream? Would anyone hear her?

"Don't do this!" she pleaded. "I like you as a teacher, but that's all—I don't feel romantic—"

Her words were cut short when he covered her mouth with a deep, long, warm kiss. She struggled to free her herself, but he was too strong.

"Mr. Phillips please stop—you're hurting me!".

Clive Phillips was forty-three years old and had never been involved in an intimate relationship with a woman. As he passionately embraced the young girl before him, he lost all sense of time, place, and propriety.

"Mr. Phillips, please stop! Please!" she cried desperately.

He pushed her back onto a stack of old band uniforms and pulled up her dress. He tore her underpants off and unfastened and pulled down his trousers with the urgency of a newlywed. He mounted her and continued to kiss her as he fumbled with her breasts. Paralyzed and numb with shock, Cheryl shut her eyes tightly and tears leaked out and slid down her cheeks. Thunder drummed across the night sky and the rain began to fall in a torrential staccato as the couples in the gymnasium danced on and Clive Phillips violated the most sacred trust given to a teacher—that of protecting the young people entrusted to him. He raped the girl.

11

"What began as a warm spring day has now quickly taken on a darker tone. We've gone from a few showers to strong thunderstorms as a cold front approaches. It looks like the Chicago area will be ground zero for a round of strong thunderstorms overnight. As of right now there are no watches or warnings in effect but there were two confirmed tornado touchdowns in eastern Iowa earlier today. We'll watch this situation and if anything severe develops we'll let you know."

—Harry Volkman, the "dean" of Chicago meteorologists

By eight-thirty Tucker Boatman was bored and had just about had his fill of the Musicians' Ball. Maybe he could talk Jeanine into going home. He was tired of making small talk with teachers and the other parents drinking punch. In fact, he wished he had something a little punchier to drink.

"I'm gonna hit the can and then we can get out of here," he said to his wife when he finally tracked her down. "Cheryl can catch a ride home with one of her friends. I'll just let her know we're gonna split." Without waiting for a reply, he headed out of the gym.

The storm outside had intensified. This was tornado season and it was starting to look like one of those nights when one could hit.

Tucker finished his business in the restroom and stepped back into the gym, looking for his daughter, but she was nowhere to be seen. He spotted Chuck Malinsky, her last dance partner, and beckoned him over.

"Hey kiddo," Tucker said. "You seen Cheryl?"

"No, sir, not since we danced a while ago," the boy answered. "She said something about getting another pair of shoes from the auditorium, but I haven't seen her since."

Tucker thanked him and headed for the auditorium. He looked into the darkened auditorium, becoming increasingly annoyed. He really wanted to go home, where he could kick back with a beer and the Bulls game.

"Cheryl," he called out as he walked down the aisle toward the stage. "You in here?"

Dammit, where was that kid? he thought. *I'd really like to catch the game before the third quarter.*

"Cheryl? Where are you?"

Nothing.

Tucker went up the stairs to the stage and walked around to the back. A faint noise reached his ears.

"Cheryl?"

He listened more closely. He could hear the faint strains of music from the gymnasium, but this sound was different, like a whimpering or crying, as if someone were hurt. It seemed to come from behind a door further backstage, and he edged closer. Yes, it definitely was someone crying—and something else. He eased the door open, and couldn't believe what he saw.

A large bolt of lightning stabbed through the darkness, illuminating the hall and the storeroom, lending a surreal cast to the image of Clive Phillips, his pants around his ankles, standing over Cheryl, who huddled on the stack of uniforms, crying. Phillips spun around as Tucker Boatman stormed into the room, grabbing the teacher by the hair and smashing him in the jaw.

"You pervert! I'll kill you!" he bellowed as he knocked Phillips to the floor.

Cheryl, already traumatized by her experience, was horrified by the violence. "Daddy, no! Stop it!" she screamed. She knew the middle-aged high school teacher would be no match for her father's brawn. Tucker Boatman was oblivious to her cries, though, and cursing, he continued to pummel Clive Phillips.

Cheryl's screams reached the gymnasium, and soon hands were pulling the two men apart. The festive mood of the evening was shattered as a crowd gathered, whispering in bewilderment at the sight of the bloodied orchestra instructor, the insanely enraged father, and the bruised and weeping girl.

The police were called and statements taken. Cheryl was taken to the hospital and given a thorough exam and rape counseling and then released to her parents. Tucker Boatman, for once having no fear of the law, gathered his wife and daughter and took them back to the relative safety of their home. Clive Phillips, twenty-two-year veteran of the Newville School system, also was taken to the hospital, but in handcuffs. His wounds would heal, but his career was shattered beyond repair.

Denise shook her head as she read over the police report of the rape incident. In her statement, Cheryl had told the police that Clive Phillips had forced himself on her, and that she had given him no encouragement whatsoever. The girl had a reputation for being somewhat shy, and didn't flirt even with boys her own age. She was definitely not a Lolita.

Denise knew that her case for the Newville school board was weak, and that she would need to really hustle in order to keep this case out of court. She still had an ace in the hole, though, and knew exactly who to call. Bert Chambers, a less-than-scrupulous reporter with the *Newville Times Bulletin*, was on his way out the door when his phone rang. He sighed. The last thing he wanted to do was take another order for a garage sale ad.

This job with the *Times Bulletin* was a far cry from the height of investigative reporting, where he had thought his journalism degree would carry him, but it was still a job, and a man had to eat, especially a two-hundred-and-fifty-plus-pound man such as he. Besides, the paper did have a large circulation, and his twice-weekly column, "Inside Whispers," was popular, making him a local celebrity. So he answered the phone. His mood brightened when he heard Denise Ryland's voice.

"Hey, Neesey, what's shakin'?" he asked.

"Same old, same old, Bert. How are things with you?"

"Ditto," he said. "What can I do for you?"

"I need you to do a story. I'll give you all the information you need for it. And don't worry," she said as he started to interrupt, "it's accurate. You can verify it if it makes you feel better. But I need this done in a hurry. As always, I'll remember you when you need me. Just make sure it gets printed."

Chambers owed Denise for several debts, and this wouldn't be the first time she'd called in some of those markers. The last time he'd aided her—in that case by using his reporter's "judgment" not to print—was during the Miller Street Bridge case. He had uncovered some information that could have sunk the deal for Denise, namely that tearing down the old bridge and putting in the strip mall would surely destroy the old Millburgh district, but he kept mum.

Luckily for Denise, no one else in the media had picked up on the potential damage losing the bridge could do until it was a done deal. In exchange for Bert Chambers' restraint, she had provided him some free but extremely valuable legal representation in some very questionable scrapes. Tit for tat, as Mama would say.

This time, she told Chambers, she had some information on the Newville school board lawsuit. He listened to what she had and agreed to print some of the juicy—and pertinent—bits in "Inside Whispers."

He immediately went to work on the story. He called Denise twice to make sure the story was angled exactly the way she wanted. Since the Sunday readership was the largest of the week, he planned to run the story then, right on the inside of the front page. Two weeks had gone by since the rape had occurred and Denise knew that she was running out of time. The media had already broken the story, and soon any chance she had of quickly settling the case would be ruined.

Denise's next call was to the attorney representing the Boatman family. As luck would have it, it was her old friend Jacob Hamilton. They hadn't spoken since the settlement of the Richards divorce case. His former paramour, Linda Richards, was finally out of his life, on the prowl for a new sweetie who could set her up in the former lifestyle to which she'd become accustomed.

Denise and Jake chitchatted for a while, then Denise brought up the Newville School Board lawsuit. He told her that he had advised the family to settle out of court, rather than put their daughter through additional trauma. The only obstacle was Tucker Boatman; he was out for blood, and refused to consider anything that would deprive him of his day in court. Denise and Hamilton both agreed that the amount the family was demanding was excessive. Knowing Denise and what she was capable of when she got into a court battle, he tried to get a feel for what she might have in store.

"If there was any way we could convince Mr. Boatman to soften his stance, you know I'd do it," he ventured.

"Everyone has a weak spot, Jake," Denise responded. "You should do everything in your power to get them to take it under advisement."

"You've got something up your sleeve," he said, his voice now less friendly.

"You know how I operate," she told him. "I'm not in this profession to win popularity contests. So we'll both just have to keep working and hope something breaks."

12

June 1998
Case Number 720018

"Still two weeks to go until summer officially begins but somebody forgot to tell Mother Nature. Today we'll get a preview of the hot, sticky season to come. The humidity will be in the sixty to seventy percent range, and that will make today's high of eighty-five feel like temperatures in the mid-nineties. Oh, the joy of summer in Chicago! The only relief we'll get today will be in the form of a few pop-up thunderstorms scattered about the area. If you get any rain, you'll be one of the lucky ones!"

—Jim Ramsey Channel 9 News

Tucker Boatman pulled the Sunday *Times Bulletin* from the mailbox. He wasn't a daily reader, but he liked to sit on the porch on Sunday mornings and have a smoke while going over the sports pages.

He sat down on the glider and glanced over the front page while he took a drink of coffee and lit a cigarette. War in eastern Europe, war in Africa, civil unrest in southeast Asia. Nothing interesting. Tucker turned to the second page and started reading "Inside Whispers." That was more like it: A gossipy, unattributed, and unaccountable column of yellow journalism, it offered little tidbits about this one and that one, and occasionally a healthy heap of mud slung here or there. Typically a fun column to read, he could usually count on it to take his mind off his own problems.

But not today. Leading this was this:

"In a sexual assault case involving a local teacher and student and about to come to trial, an interesting piece of information has surfaced. The girl's stepfather . . ."

When he saw his old Chicago PD mug shot on the page, he was livid. The scar on his face seemed more menacing, and he could hardly believe that the cold, dark eyes staring at him from the newspaper were in fact his own.

Numb with shock, he read the story containing the old child molestation charge. He thought that he had put that behind him, but there, in black and white, were all the sordid details including his arrest and prison record. The article carried a snide tone, as if someone who knew him well but who didn't like him very much had written it. He could see where this could lead; with such a story out, it could be inferred that he perhaps had sexually abused Cheryl, and that his claim against the school and the school board were just a smokescreen designed to cover up his own guilt.

He couldn't belileve it. All of the hard work he had done to become the image of a model citizen was for nothing. His past scrapes had caused them to have to move and start from nothing, and it had almost destroyed his marriage. Years of struggle to establish a normal life were down the drain. Now everything lay in ruins.

Denise Ryland normally started her Sunday with the *New York Times* crossword puzzle. She never was able to finish one, but she sometimes got close. Growing up in Mississippi, she had always fantasized about living in a big city like New York, and reading the *Times* gave her a feeling of connection to the Big Apple. When Jerry had been offered the job in Chicago, it was she who had insisted that he take it. Nothing excited her more than the fast-paced city lifestyle.

Driving through a sleepy little bedroom community like Newville was the last thing she wanted to do on a lovely spring Sunday morning, but here she was. Bert Chambers had faxed her a copy of the story exactly as it would appear in the paper. It was written exactly as she had wanted, but now she needed to confirm that it was indeed printed, and it couldn't wait until Monday.

She stopped at the Wilco Drugstore and Diner in downtown Newville and ordered breakfast and bought a copy of the *Newville Times Bulletin*. She wasn't hungry, but it would give her a chance to read the story on Tucker Boatman.

As Bert Chambers had been instructed, and he had promised, it was a sad saga indeed. Anyone reading the story would feel that Tucker Boatman's influence on Cheryl or anyone else was a bad one. And who could tell what had gone on inside the Boatman home, or how it had contributed to the girl's sexual attitudes? Perfect. It was exactly the kind of tempest Hurricane Denise wanted to have stirred up. Satisfied with the article, Denise paid for her breakfast, tucked the paper under her arm, and went to her car. Going by directions Bert Chambers had given her, she drove past the Boatman family home.

There on the front porch on the glider, his head in hands, sat Tucker Boatman, a portrait in misery. Denise slowed to get a closer look. He didn't look nearly as menacing in person as he did in the paper, but they never did. She decided against getting out of the car and facing him in person, so she drove around the corner, pulled over, and made a call from her cell phone.

"Tucker Boatman, please," Denise said to the woman who answered the phone.

She watched as a woman came out and handed Tucker the cordless phone. He seemed oblivious to her, and she had to shake him by the shoulder to get his attention.

"Yeah?" he said gruffly when he answered.

"How do you like having your name in the paper again, Mr. Boatman?" Denise asked.

"What the—" he sputtered. "Who is this?"

"Settle your case with the school board out of court, or this is just the beginning," she replied. "It would be a shame to drag your entire family through the mud."

"Who the hell is this?" Tucker screamed, but the only sound he heard was the annoying hum of the dial tone.

As Denise watched, Tucker Boatman angrily threw the receiver into the yard. It split into pieces and he stormed inside the house, slamming the screen door behind him. Her work here being done, she drove on through the town and cruised by the high school. With a pang, she wistfully looked at the schoolyard, wondering whether she would see a child of her own at play. Since her miscarriage, she'd felt a nagging sense of responsibility for losing the baby, despite the doctor's reassurances. Even though in her mind she knew she could conceive again, deep in her heart she feared she'd never have another chance to have a child. The thought that she might not be worthy of raising a child flitted through her mind occasionally, like a little ghost, but she forced herself to quickly dismiss the notion.

On Monday, Denise began her day with her usual five-mile run. She got home and headed for a quick shower, but her suddenly amorous husband diverted her to the bedroom. Being a partner does have its advantages, she thought as he peeled off her sweat-drenched sports bra and shorts. She would arrive at the office a little later than she wanted to, but this was well worth it.

As she passed her secretary's desk, Lisa handed her a stack of pink message slips. Client, client, client—and one not from a client, but from Jacob Hamilton. Going into her office, she set down her briefcase and called him. Tucker Boatman had called him the day before, he told her. Suddenly it seemed that Mr. Boatman was in a very agreeable mood.

The proposal she offered was instantly accepted. Within two hours the paperwork was signed and the deal was made. The Boatmans were given enough to make their lives quite comfortable, albeit not filthy rich, and the Newville School Board was saved from a terrible legal and public relations problem. Most importantly, the lawsuit was settled according to Denise Ryland's terms.

Another client's needs had been met. Hurricane Denise had moved in, flipped over the requisite trailer park, flattened another town, and left the survivors to clean up the mess in her wake.

13

A week later, on the very last day of school in Newville, Jacob Hamilton called Denise with the news. It would be on the evening news, but he wanted to tell her himself.

Still distraught over the incident at the Musician's Ball, Cheryl hadn't returned to school, and her mother had been unable to get her to even come out of her room for several days. The family was falling to pieces. Jeanine's whole life had revolved around her daughter and it was tearing her apart to see the girl so depressed. Of course her mother knew Cheryl was not to blame for what had happened to her. She was a victim.

Jeanine had tried to get Cheryl to talk, but the only response she got was a mumbled apology for embarrassing them. Her flute remained in its case. She couldn't bear to look at it, much less play it.

Tucker Boatman's fury over the rape of his daughter and his distress over the newspaper article had subsided. Knowing the lawsuit had been settled and that the family would soon be receiving a considerable sum of money had gone a long way in bringing him to a much calmer state. As it turned out, few people in the community had read the article, and even fewer paid much attention to it. Despite the inferences it had made, it nonetheless had stated clearly that his former record was much in the past, and the hint of child molestation from years before was groundless. Cheryl's parents decided to let her stay home for a few more days, and then, pointing out that life went on regardless, Tucker insisted that she go for the last day of school.

Gathering all the courage she could muster, Cheryl Boatman obeyed her stepfather's wishes, even though the last thing in the world she wanted to do was return to the site of so much agony. She didn't see how she could ever face her friends again, and the coming summer vacation that she had so looked forward to was certain to be a disaster. She knew that the school had been in an uproar over the whole incident and Mr. Phillips' subsequent arrest and dismissal. She was sure everyone blamed her.

She dressed quietly that morning, putting on a mint-green shirtwaist dress that her mother had made for her. Green was Cheryl's favorite color, and maybe wearing it would give her courage. Checking herself in the mirror, she carefully adjusted her belt, made sure all the buttons were all fastened, and smoothed the skirt. She hadn't had much of an appetite lately, so she skipped breakfast. Unable to look her parents in the eye, she murmured a good-bye, picked up her books, and walked out the door and down the sidewalk with her head down.

Instead of taking the schoolbus, she opted to walk to school, thereby hoping to avoid facing her classmates for as long as possible. With tears in her eyes, Jeanine watched her daughter head slowly toward the school; if only there was something she could do to help her get over this.

The bell was ringing by the time Cheryl got to school. She dawdled for a while at her locker, then, for the first time in her life, she decided to skip her first class and went instead to the girl's restroom. She stood before the mirror for several minutes, examining her reflection.

She didn't like the face that looked back at her. All she saw was a troublemaker. For years, she had blamed herself for insisting on having a sleepover for her ninth birthday party, even though her parents had been reluctant to have so many children in so small a house. But she had thrown a tantrum and her mother had given in, and talked her stepfather into agreeing. And because of that, her stepfather had been put in that horrible position and they'd had to move.

Now there was this awful situation with poor Mr. Phillips. He had been so kind to her, and had taken so much time and effort to give her the flute lessons. She must have done something wrong, because he had told her that she was too irresistible. Now his life was destroyed, and that was all her fault too. It was no wonder her biological father had abandoned her as a baby and had never wanted her or even contacted her. She was a miserable excuse for a human being.

Cheryl neatly set her books on the floor by the wall where no one would stumble over them, and placed her purse on top. She took off her shoes and set them by the stack. With an elastic band, she pulled her hair back into a ponytail so it wouldn't be in the way, and then went into a stall and locked the door. She slipped her belt off and, carefully balancing herself, stood on the toilet seat. A steam pipe ran just above the stalls, and Cheryl tossed the buckle end of the belt over the pipe. Balancing precariously on her tiptoes, she pulled the belt through the buckle, tied a loop in the belt with a slip knot, and slid it over her head. Making sure the knot was tight and the loop was secure, she stepped off the toilet seat. When the first-period class ended, two girls, giggling and chattering, came into the restroom and discovered a horrific sight. Paramedics were called and CPR was administered, but it was too late.

For the first time in her career, Denise took the rest of the day off. She couldn't concentrate, and was filled with a profound sadness brought on by a deep sense of guilt. Dear God, what had she done? That poor girl had been an innocent pawn caught in the midst of legal wrangling and public scrutiny as complicated and brutal as a television wrestling match. With both sides focusing on depositions, outmaneuvering each other, and how many billable hours they could rack up, no one noticed a young girl quietly anguishing. The ultimate cost was too high. She knew in her heart that she had been wrong.

In a fog, she somehow made her way home, where she turned on the television. She flipped through the channels over and over until finally she found a news report on the tragedy. She sat in numb silence as the reporter on the scene gave the details of the suicide.

Before her eyes flashed scenes of the school, grieving classmates being helped into cars by heartbroken parents, and an interview with the principal, who described Cheryl as one of their finest pupils. This was devastating to the whole community. The reporter gave a brief review of Tucker Boatman's troubles, and a videotaped clip of Clive Phillips being led away in handcuffs was shown along with a reference to the lawsuit and settlement. And then, the most heart-wrenching picture of all: a gurney carrying Cheryl Boatman's body-bagged form being loaded into an ambulance. Flashing back to the station, the noon anchor closed the story, with the image of Cheryl's smiling freshman class picture featured in the background, then the screen dipped to black.

As Denise watched the report, tears stung her eyes. Shutting the TV off, she leaned her head back and covered her face with her hands. She jumped as the shrilling of the telephone pierced the silence. Taking a deep breath, she answered, annoyed to find that the caller was Linda Richards. How in the world had she gotten her home number? The woman's voice rang with hatred.

"You snake, what a poor excuse for a woman you are. You killed that kid in Newville. She committed suicide because of you. I know how you operate, putting that little item in the newspaper."

"What are you talking about?" Denise said. "You don't know anyth—"

Richards cut her off. "Like hell I don't," she snapped. "You forget what a small world the legal community is. Word gets around. I have my own sources, you know, and I know how you got that reporter in Newville to print the story just so you could get that lawsuit settled your way—just like I know your phone number and where you live. Well, I hope you're happy now, because that poor little girl suffered, and you just took advantage of it. Now she's dead because of you and her blood is on your hands—"

Denise hung up the phone. She didn't need Linda Richards to

point out her shortcomings, or her guilt. She went to the kitchen and got a glass of water, then went back into the living room, pulled the shades closed and sat down. Rubbing her temples with her fingertips, she considered the underhanded tactics she used to win cases, and the many ways she had circumvented the truth. Crooked deals she had brokered filed through her mind like a parade of dragons. In her quest to get to the top and become a partner she had always been willing to capitalize on any weakness she found in her adversaries, even if it meant compromising her own ethics. Winning the case, coming out on top—nothing had mattered more than that. Everything else had been secondary.

She had lost a child and almost lost her own life because of her relentless drive to climb to the top of her profession. Now her win-at-all-cost mentality had claimed another victim. No longer could she rationalize her actions, justify them as being a necessary part of her job. What Linda Richards had said cut through her heart, because it was true.

She was responsible for Cheryl Boatman's death as surely as if she had tied the noose herself. She had traded her soul for a partnership.

Denise slumped in her chair, and silent tears flowed.

When Jerry got home that evening, he was surprised to find his wife already there. Denise was lying on the bed, pretending to sleep, and he sat next to her.

"You okay, baby?" he asked her, his voice concerned. "It's not like you to be home this early in the day."

"I'm all right. I just had a headache and decided to knock off early." She couldn't bring herself to talk about the suicide just yet.

He kissed her cheek, then went to the basement to do his exercises. She lay on the bed a few minutes longer, then got up and went to the bathroom. There, she studied her reflection in the medicine-cabinet mirror.

The image looking back at her was ashen and pale. That wouldn't do at all, she thought, and splashed cold water on her face. She went to the kitchen and poured a glass of orange juice, then went to the basement to watch Jerry work out. He was in the middle of a set of bicep curls, but he took one look at her and knew something was wrong.

"Denise, what is it?" he asked, and she burst into tears.

He lifted her up and carried her upstairs to bed. He held her tightly and consoled her until the storm passed, and she finally slept. As she drifted off, she thought that if Denise Ryland still had a soul, perhaps she could reclaim it in the safe harbor of her husband's love.

Later that night, as Jerry snored softly beside her, she lay awake and stared into the darkness. Hurricane Denise had finally blown herself out. That cold and calculating woman had died that day, along with Cheryl Boatman. In the midnight silence her mother's words came back to her: "From where your treasure is, there will your heart be also, and what does it profit a man to gain the whole world, if he loses his own soul?" Mama had often said that, but that wasn't another one of her aphorisms. This saying was from the Bible, and Denise now knew it was true.

She thought of her lost baby and asked herself, "Would I be the kind of mother a child could be proud of?" As the question whirled around in her mind, the answer came to her. She also knew what she had to do.

She rose early the next day, and foregoing her usual run, she dressed in blue jeans and a T-shirt and went to her office. There she typed her resignation, cleaned out her desk, and left the law offices of Fisk and Ryan forever.

Denise spent the next few days at home wallowing in guilt and self-pity, but that soon wore thin. Mama had not raised her to be a whiner and a moper, so Denise began making plans to change her life. She still loved the law, but was determined that she would never practice it as she had before. Instead, she would dedicate herself to the kind of law her father had practiced, helping the poor, needy souls who helplessly clung to the edges of the criminal justice system. He had been a county prosecutor before becoming a judge, and died when she was eleven years old. He had never made much money, but he was well-loved and respected in their hometown, and she had always been proud of him.

Denise joined a less prestigious but honorable law firm that respected her desire to do a certain amount of *pro bono* cases for individuals who needed help but couldn't afford to pay. Her personal payday was beyond value: For the first time in as long as she could remember, her empty soul began to fill back up with pride and self-worth.

Another bonus was that she had more time to spend with Jerry. He started accompanying her on her morning runs, and she joined him in the evenings for some weight lifting. Emotionally and physically, she felt healthier than ever.

About two months later, Denise's appetite started to drop off. Normally, she doted on steaks and thick grilled burgers, but suddenly she couldn't stand the sight or the smell of them. Oddly, though, she found herself eating hot dogs and bologna sandwiches just for the yellow mustard she slathered on till it dripped onto the plate. To make matters worse, she couldn't sit down for more than five minutes without dozing off.

Figuring she was dealing with a mild bug, she ignored the symptoms until one morning she got up and almost didn't make it to the bathroom before puking. Alarmed, Jerry insisted she see a doctor—now. Sick and tired of feeling sick and tired, she didn't argue, and to the doctor she went. The doctor ran a few tests, checked her over thoroughly, and smiled and patted her hand. Not to worry, he told her; lots of women had these symptoms when they were expecting a baby.

14

The woman dressed as a flight attendant was aggravated that the uniform felt so tight, and at first, it had made her uncomfortable. Lately she had been depressed and had gained some weight, and the timing couldn't have been worse. Flight attendants were usually pretty slim, and she felt that her chunkiness drew too much attention to her. Normally, with her glasses on, and her weight down, no one ever noticed her. Still, she told herself, there was no way she could back out now. There was too much at stake. Besides, today was going to be *her* day.

After a while, she began to enjoy the men ogling her. She smiled coyly as she moved past them, and her walk became a breezy stroll. She was transformed from a slightly too-round woman with low self-esteem into someone who felt confident and beautiful. She liked feeling that way again.

It was a lovely early summer morning, and after she had left the hotel, walking through the streets of downtown Chicago, she felt the energy of the city as if for the first time. She breathed deeply, then, vibrant and radiating confidence, she boarded the train to O'Hare.

Upon entering the airport, her confidence waned. Again, she felt conspicuous. Nervously, she hurried into the ladies' room, where she combed her hair and touched up her lipstick. She was beginning to flush, and she forced herself to calm down.

"You can do this," she said as looked at her reflection in the mirror.

She had never truly believed she could go through with the plan, and now her nerves were starting to get the better of her. The stress made her feel the need to urinate, and she stepped into a stall and carefully locked the door behind her. As she sat there, she fished in her purse for a cigarette. Disregarding the no-smoking sign, she lit up anyway. After four or five drags she felt better and flushed the cigarette down the toilet. She waited in the stall until a few more women had come and gone—who could prove which one had been the smoker?—and came out of the stall. Giving her hair one last touch-up, she left the restroom and moved quickly toward the gate. As she approached her destination, she was startled by what she saw, even though she'd expected it. There was Denise Ryland with her baby and her husband. Her steps faltered, then she regained her composure.

"Follow the plan!" she told herself sternly.

Clutching her forged identification card, she surreptitiously watched the Rylands. Jerry had his arm around Denise and was handing her a cup of coffee. Rage waved over her, making her want to pounce on Denise Ryland and throw the hot coffee in her face. No! She couldn't blow it now. She wouldn't let anything spoil her plan—she had waited too long. Not wanting to be spotted by them, she turned and walked toward the gate attendant, and reported for duty.

"Hi, there, um—" She craned to get a look at the counter attendant's name tag. "—Jason! Hi, there, Jason. I'm Alice Metliff." She smiled uneasily as she held the fake ID out to him. "I'm working the flight to L.A."

"Just a sec', Alice," Jason said, holding up one finger. He was busy checking the schedule on the computer and barely gave her a nod. A few anxious moments went by while she waited. She had been told to expect to be escorted to the plane with no problem, so she forced herself to remain calm.

"Okay, Alice," he finally said. "Let me check your ID."

Remaining poised, she handed him the card. He swiped it across the scanner, frowned, and swiped it again.

"That's weird," he said. "Your aircraft access card doesn't seem to be scanning. Have you been having any trouble with it lately?" He eyed her cautiously.

Her heart thudded, and panic was making her knees wobbly.

"Well, no . . . no, not really, but . . . You know what?" she stammered. "This sounds so stupid, but I accidentally left it with my uniform when I washed it, and it went through both the washer and the dryer." She smiled self-deprecatingly. "Do you suppose I fried it?"

"Hey, if I had a dollar for every time I've done that, I wouldn't still need to be working here," he laughed. "Tell you what—let me try something else . . ."

She held her breath as he turned the card so that the magnetic stripe faced the other way. He swiped the card again and this time the scanner beeped. Jason entered a few items into the computer, then led her over to the locked corridor and opened the door to let her in.

"Fly safe, Alice, and have a good day," he said, as he watched her walk down the aisle.

"You too, Jason," she said, breathing a sigh of relief.

She'd always considered herself to be a good actress; now she would see if she could pull off the role of a lifetime. Once inside the aircraft, she introduced herself to the flight crew. She knew that in order for the plan to work, she had to convince them that she was who she claimed to be.

"Hi, I'm Alice Metliff, senior on-call flight attendant. Cathy Thompson called in sick and I'm filling in for her today," she said to the pilot.

"Hi, Alice. George Middleton. I hope it's nothing serious," the pilot responded as he shook her hand.

"I'm sure it's just a twenty-four-hour bug."

She introduced herself to the rest of the flight crew and began to perform her pre-flight checklist duties. She tried to remember everything she'd read in the stolen manuals, and that her expert coach had told her, and began to prepare for boarding.

15

Three hours into her trip, Denise had been sitting comfortably in the window seat, with her book in her lap, dozing. The baby, asleep in her carrier, was in the aisle seat. The woman who called herself Alice Metliff had had the unexpected good luck of not only working in the first-class cabin, but also being able to become familiar with Denise and her baby. Denise had even asked her to watch the baby while she went to the restroom. Other passengers, if they had paid attention, would have seen that the young mother trusted her. Still, she felt that Denise and everybody else was watching her. No question about it, she was very self-conscious, and was afraid it would show. Now her moment had come, her chance to act, and at the last minute she was having to force herself to carry the plan through.

Leaning over toward Denise, she lightly touched her on the shoulder and asked, "Ma'am, can I bring you something else to drink?" She smiled sweetly. She had been rehearsing this part for days.

"A glass of water would be great, thanks," Denise replied.

She had hoped Denise would ask for a flavored drink, but water would have to do. Hopefully a couple of lemon wedges would be sufficient. At the flight attendant's serving station, struggling to hold her hands steady, she dumped a small packet of powder into Denise's drink and stirred it.

"Thank you," Denise said as took the glass. The woman watched her drink the liquid, and was gratified to see that within a few minutes Denise was becoming quite drowsy.

The pilot's voice came over the intercom. "Good afternoon, ladies and gentlemen. We are now in California. Those are the San Gabriel Mountains below us . . ." As he continued, describing weather in Los Angeles and approximate arrival time, the woman watched Denise drift off into sleep.

Now! The time had come to strike! This was truly a moment for celebration. For so long she had been unable to think of anything else. Now she could do what she had spent months preparing for.

Standing just in front of the cockpit, she carefully examined the passengers in the first-class cabin. They were either sleeping or engrossed in books or laptop computers. She walked up and down the aisle once, appearing to check to see if anyone needed anything. She was relieved that that pesky red-haired woman was sound asleep, snoring, a little bead of drool slithering down her chin. She had shown such an interest in the baby, she could have been trouble. Glancing around once more to be sure no one was paying attention to her, the attendant gently lifted the baby from the travel carrier. She spied the stuffed bunny in the carrier and quickly bundled the bunny under the blanket and left it behind.

So far, so good! The baby hadn't cried! she thought.

She conspicuously pulled a diaper out of the baby bag in case someone should notice her. Anyone watching would assume that she was going to change the baby for the mother. That story would also cover her if Denise Ryland should happen to awake—helpful little flight attendant aiding a resting mother. She calmly moved to the flight attendant's serving station with the baby in her arms. Taking a small vial from her purse, she used a medicine dropper and gave the baby a small dose of the drug she'd given Denise. She had to be sure the baby slept until they arrived in Los Angeles and were away from the airport. Taking a quick look around, she then quietly placed the baby inside a large bag she'd brought with her and had stashed in the garment storage area. She arranged a blanket over the sleeping infant and left the bag unzipped so the child could breathe easily. Satisfied that the most difficult part of her mission was accomplished, she puttered around the serving station and waited for the plane to begin its descent. Luckily for her, Cathy Thompson was new to this flight crew, so her absence hadn't seemed unusual. Substitute attendants were always coming into the stewarding pool, or so she had been told. The other flight attendants were busy at the rear of the aircraft, so she didn't have to worry about getting involved in a shop-talk conversation where she might be found out.

"Ladies and gentleman," the pilot announced, "due to some heavy traffic at LAX, we're going to have to wait for clearance to land. The delay shouldn't be more than fifteen minutes or so."

As she went through the cabin reminding passengers to fasten their seatbelts and close their tray tables, her anxiety grew. Any delay increased the risk of her plan failing. She was so close, and now that she had her prize, she wanted nothing more than to get off the plane and get away. Before she took her seat in preparation for landing, she peeked inside the bag; the tiny girl slept peacefully.

She began to fret about everything that could go wrong. How long would the drug she had given Denise and the baby last? What if Denise woke up? What if the baby woke up and began to cry?

The thought of going to prison for attempted kidnapping terrified her. The minutes dragged by. After about fifteen minutes she leaned over and peeked into the bag again. The baby slept still, her breathing slow and even. Twenty minutes passed, and beads of sweat dotted the woman's forehead. Finally, the pilot made another announcement.

"Ladies and gentleman, we have received clearance to land. Please be sure your seatbelts are fastened in preparation for landing, and thank you for flying West Lines Air."

The touchdown was smooth and uneventful. Denise stirred once and her eyelids fluttered, then with a sigh she continued to sleep. The plane taxied into the terminal and the woman anxiously waited. Both Denise Ryland and the baby remained quiet as the plane came to a complete stop. After taking a moment to calm herself, the woman quickly opened the airplane exit door exactly as she had been instructed. It was as if she had done it for years.

"Hey, can you give me a hand?" she said as she handed her flight manifest passenger data to the counter attendant waiting to greet the plane. "I've got an international flight to Tokyo and our delay in landing has made me late. If you deplane for me, I can just about make it to the international terminal."

"No problem. Where's Cathy? I thought she was doing this flight," the counter attendant said.

"Oh, she was sick—some kind of bug—and asked me to sub for her," she said breezily as she carefully removed her prize from the garment storage area. One quick glance showed her Denise was still asleep as people stood around her. But she didn't have time to congratulate herself. Any minute now the drug would wear off.

"By the way, I'm Alice," she said to the gate attendant. "I really appreciate this. I owe you one." The gate attendant stepped onto the plane, and as the passengers gathered their belongings and lined up to disembark, the woman started down the jetway to the terminal, unnoticed, taking the most precious part of Denise Ryland's life with her.

16

When Los Angeles Airport Police responded to a distress call on flight 471 from Chicago, they entered into a chaotic situation of grumbling passengers, a flustered flight crew, and a worried airline PR executive. At the center of the uproar was a frantic mother whose eight-week-old baby was missing.

The atmosphere on the plane was becoming increasingly volatile as the minutes passed. Until the crisis was resolved one way or another, everyone on board was confined to the aircraft, and many of the passengers had connecting flights to catch. Although they were sympathetic to the situation, to say they were upset at the delay was an understatement. Compounding the problem, since the plane had landed, the air conditioning had been shut off, and the stale air inside the plane was heating up along with the tempers.

The plane had been turned inside out, but no trace of the baby could be found. Faced with the almost certain likelihood that a kidnapping had occurred, the airport police called the Los Angeles Police Department and the FBI.

LAPD detectives Kyle Berryman and Dave Roberts responded to the call. They had never handled nor even heard of case like this; it was very unusual, even for Los Angeles. They reviewed the findings—or lack thereof—with the airport police, and then began their own search.

Berryman and Roberts checked over the flight manifest and then did a head count. Somehow, ten passengers had managed to slip past the guards and departed the aircraft, further complicating the investigation. One of the flight attendants was gone, also. The detectives talked with the remaining passengers and flight crew, and after a thorough check of identification and carry-on baggage, and promising to have their checked luggage forwarded as quickly as possible, they were allowed to go on their way.

Now, the detectives were faced with interrogating the mother. They escorted her into the terminal and to a small flight-crew lounge where they could conduct their interview in private.

Detectives typically dreaded having to question women in missing-child cases. They were usually extremely emotional and often unable to provide much information or help, and most of the time was spent just trying to calm them down. However, no detective had ever dealt with the type of woman that was Denise Ryland.

Detective Berryman introduced himself and began. "Ma'am, I know you've suffered a terrible blow here today, but I'm here to help you find your child," he said, and braced himself for the anticipated outburst of tears.

By now, however, although she was still upset and teary, Denise was past hysterics. Logic told her that her baby could not possibly have vanished into thin air, and her analytical mind was at work trying to fit the pieces of the puzzle together.

Meanwhile, Berryman's partner, Dave Roberts, and two other LAPD officers searched the plane again, inch by inch. Knowing that they needed to work quickly before the trail grew cold, they opened and examined the checked-in bags of each person on the flight. They got the phone numbers and addresses of the ten passengers and the flight attendant who had departed the aircraft before their arrival, and started making calls.

In the lounge, Berryman and Denise continued their interview. Despite her relatively calm demeanor, her nerves were stretched to the snapping point, and she found Berryman's presence comforting. He was a gray-haired, grandfatherly man with heavy eyebrows and a gentle expression, and as they talked, she grew to believe that if anyone could find her Rachel, he would.

"We've searched every millimeter of the plane and gone through all the baggage," he said. "There doesn't seem to be any trace of the baby. Is there anything you can think of that you may not have told us, Mrs. Ryland?" He looked deep into her eyes.

"I've told you everything I can think of," she answered. "Wait a minute—surely you don't think *I* did something to my baby!"

"Mrs. Ryland, in a case like this, we have to examine all the possibilities. I'm not accusing you, but you have to look at it from our point of view."

With her years of experience in the legal field, she knew he was right; the first suspects in missing-child cases were always the parents. Sighing, she told her story again, from the time she first boarded until she awoke after the plane had landed.

"Do you remember anyone showing any particular interest in the baby?" he asked. Denise sighed. Rachel was a beautiful baby, and people were always oohing and aahing over her.

"There was a woman sitting across the aisle from me, a red-haired woman," Denise answered. "She seemed nice enough, but she kind of creeped me out. She practically grabbed Rachel out of her carrier, said she had a baby granddaughter who died recently. I practically had to smack her hand away, but I can't imagine she would take her, knowing how much pain it would cause."

Berryman checked the copy of the manifest. The red-haired woman, Rhoda Mankoff, lived in a gated community in Laguna Beach. She wouldn't be hard to track down.

"We can't count on who would or wouldn't seem to be a kidnapper, Mrs. Ryland. Sometimes grief can make a person do strange things. Did anyone else seem unusual?"

Denise racked her brain. She shook her head, unable to think of anything.

There was a tapping at the door, and Dave Roberts came in.

"We managed to track down six of the passengers who got by us," Roberts said. "They were still in the airport. Missed their connecting flights. They were pretty pissed, but cooperative. They were clean."

"Swell," Berryman said. He handed a slip of paper with Rhoda

Mankoff's name and address on it to Roberts. "Here, go check this out. This gal had a real strong interest in the baby."

Roberts left, and Berryman and Denise continued to discuss the details of the flight.

"There has to be something you're missing," he said. "Let's go over it again, from the very beginning."

Denise closed her eyes, trying to capture a replay of the day. Again, she could come up with nothing unusual. Tears of frustration and worry stung her eyes.

"Okay," Berryman said. "What about food? What did you have to eat?"

Denise listed everything, from the tea and croissant she'd had before takeoff, to the eggs Benedict and fruit cup for breakfast, to the green peppercorn-encrusted beef medallions she'd had for lunch.

"What about drinks. Did you have any wine or cocktails?"

No, she hadn't, she explained, because she was nursing and couldn't drink alcohol.

"You said you took a nap. Tell me again, how long did you sleep?" he asked.

"I slept for about an hour, I think," she answered. "But when I woke up, I went to the restroom, and when I came back I checked Rachel and she was fine."

"Did you leave her alone while you went to the restroom?"

"No, of course not. I would never leave her alone in a public place, not even for a moment." A pang stabbed through her, and she caught her breath. Even with all her care, something—maybe something awful—had happened to her baby.

"So, who watched her while you were gone?"

"One of the flight attendants," Denise said. "I don't remember her name—Amy, Ann—something that began with an 'A.' "

Berryman looked over the list of the crew. None of the flight attendants' names began with A.

"Are you sure maybe the name didn't begin with another letter?" he asked.

"Dammit, yes, I'm sure! Don't you think I know how to read?" Denise snapped. This was ridiculous. How could anyone just walk out with her baby and not be noticed? Were the police in California blind? She covered her eyes with her hands.

"I'm sorry, I'm sorry," she wept. "I just want my baby back."

Kyle Berryman patted her shoulder and let her cry, waiting patiently until she regained her composure. Then he went to the refrigerator and took out a pitcher of water. Pouring two glasses full, he handed one to her. He took a sip of his and made a face.

"Hang on a minute before you drink that," he said. "The water here doesn't always taste so hot. Let me put a piece of lemon in it for you."

Emotionally drained, Denise sat numbly and studied the glass before her. Something about the lemon in the water . . .

"Alice."

"Beg pardon?"

"Alice," Denise said. "That's her name—the flight attendant."

He looked at the list of flight attendants again.

"Mrs. Ryland, there's no one on this list named Alice. Are you *sure* that was her name?"

"Yes, I'm as sure as I am of my own name. There must be a mistake on the list."

Berryman was puzzled. He picked up the phone and made a call, then hung up and pulled out a note pad.

"Can you describe the woman?"

Once again, Denise's years of legal training and attention to detail proved invaluable, and by closing her eyes and visualizing, she was able to give a very thorough description of the woman.

"One of the things that made me notice her appearance was that her uniform seemed tight on her, and I remember thinking that flight attendants didn't have to be Barbie dolls anymore," she said.

The phone rang and Berryman picked it up. He spoke in low tones for a few minutes, and Denise strained to hear what he was saying. He hung up and looked at her.

"No wonder we couldn't find her on the list," he said. "An attendant by the name of Cathy Thompson was scheduled to work this flight, but she got sick and another one subbed for her. The sub's name was penciled in but didn't get entered on the printout. Her name is Alice Metliff."

Berryman called for a sketch artist, and Denise once more described the woman called Alice Metliff. The sketch was photocopied and distributed and faxed to all LAPD officers. Denise also gave them the picture of Rachel that she carried in her wallet.

Now the detectives were faced with the question of why anyone would target Denise's baby?

Why indeed? It was a question Denise uncomfortably thought she could answer, and she began to tell Detective Berryman about all the enemies she'd collected over the years. Once again, one of Mama's sayings echoed in her mind: "As you sow, so shall you reap." After all the years of double-handed dirty dealing, and despite her reformation in the past thirteen months, she was reaping enough grief to last her for a lifetime.

She was reluctant to tell this obviously ethical man about the sordidness of her past career, but she knew it was necessary. Denise described the corners she had cut and the dirty deals she had negotiated in order to win her cases, and the lives she had destroyed in the process. Perhaps one of the people she had hurt had sought revenge and taken her child. Could it be Jimmy George Hinson, reaching from death row? His sister had sat through that trial, glaring at Denise and mouthing obscenities. Still convinced of her brother's innocence, believing he had lied in his courtroom confession simply to get it over with or to show off, she was sure he'd been railroaded and had spent every dime she had hiring lawyers to make appeal after appeal.

Maybe it was the former Linda Richards, who had been rendered divorced, penniless, and bitter, thanks to Denise. Even though she had seemingly gotten her life and her status back together, Linda was still spewing venom and hell-bent as ever on getting even.

A third guess was Tucker Boatman, whom she knew to be a violent and vengeful man. His loss had been the greatest, Denise realized, now that her own child was missing. Who else would most want her to go through that particular kind of agony?

Kyle Berryman took detailed notes, then escorted Denise to a taxi, promising that he would keep her updated on anything he found out.

Later on, alone with her thoughts in her hotel room, Denise considered everything that had happened. The ghosts of her past cases haunted her, mocking her as they flitted through her mind. Denise had become her own judge, jury, and executioner, and her guilt weighed heavily. Where had she lost her way? Would she ever be whole again? She was tormented by thoughts of what might be happening to her baby. Her breasts were hard and sore from needing to nurse her child, and her arms ached to hold her.

And what about Jerry? She been trying feverishly to call him but got no answer. He must still be at his presentation. When she talked to him, what would she say? She remembered their heartache when she had miscarried their first child, and now their precious baby girl had seemingly disappeared into thin air, possibly because of someone seeking revenge on her.

She didn't try to hold back her tears now. More than anything else she had ever wanted to do for Jerry was to give him a child. Now she had lost two of them.

17

July 1999
Los Angeles

> "Today promises to be a lovely day in the L.A. basin. You can expect sunny skies, with highs in the city near seventy, and highs well into the eighties in the Valley. Low pressure over southern Arizona will give us an easterly breeze, so we won't see as much smog as usual this afternoon. Now, if you like the red carnation on my lapel, you can get one for yourself by making a donation to the Huntington Park Nature Society."
>
> —KNBC-TV meteorologist Chris Nance

The woman calling herself Alice Metliff went into an airport ladies room and, checking to be sure she was alone, took the baby out of the bag. That was not how she'd been instructed, but it was impossible to walk through the airport carrying a baby in a bag; someone was bound to notice. She set the still-sleeping infant on the diaper changing table, then turned her attention to herself.

She pulled a blond wig out of her hand bag and carefully slipped it on, making sure none of her own hair showed. She then removed her glasses and inserted a pair of contact lenses. She finished her transformation by taking off the flight attendant's uniform and putting on a gray pantsuit. Stepping back, she examined herself in the full-length mirror. Perfect. She bore no resemblance to the woman who had so solicitously waited on Denise Ryland on the airplane.

The woman gathered up the discarded uniform and stuffed it into the bag that had held the baby, and crammed the bag into the trashcan. She slipped a blue-and-white striped sweater and cap on the baby and wrapped her in a blue blanket, taking care to cover the little face. Then she picked the child up, slung her bag over her shoulder, took a deep breath, and was on her way. She had the advantage of time, but not for long—five, ten minutes tops, while the loss was determined by the drugged woman and airport security, who must be working on the situation by now. She would have to hurry.

There was nothing remarkable about a woman walking through an airport with a baby, but she knew that by now the alarm would have been raised, and she was nervous. What if they stopped everyone with a baby? Even though she had dressed the child in a boy's outfit, one check in the diaper would give it away.

She continued down the concourse toward the taxi stand, trying to keep her gaze steady and avoid direct eye contact with anyone. She was almost to the door when she spotted a couple of policemen scanning the crowd. What could she do? She couldn't afford to be stopped now. Frantic, she looked around. Suddenly, a family of five adults and four children came up behind her, chatting with each other and engulfing her as they passed her. Seizing the opportunity, she gaily began talking and walking with them, disregarding the odd looks they gave her. Thinking she was one of the group, the police ignored her and she walked through the automatic doors and out to the taxi stand.

The woman got into one of the waiting cabs and continued to hold her breath until the vehicle pulled away and merged onto the highway. Finally, she was able to lean back and relax a little. Pulling the blanket away from the baby's face, she was relieved to see that the child still slept. She hoped she hadn't given her too much of the drug, and lightly tickled the infant's face. The child puckered up a little and made a little mewling noise, then opened her eyes. The woman panicked a bit—she wasn't prepared to feed the baby just yet, but relaxed when she rubbed her eyes and went back to sleep.

She looked up and saw that the cab driver was looking at her in the rearview mirror.

"That sure is a pretty baby," he said. "How old is he?"

"He's, um, he's four months old," she answered.

"Really? Kinda small for four months, ain't he?" the driver said. "Ah, but what I know about babies you could put in your hand. Sure is a cute little fella, though."

She thanked him, wishing he would just pay attention to his driving and leave her alone. It made her nervous to have someone pay that much attention to her and the baby. He yammered on for a while longer, but when she made it clear she had no interest in conversation, he finally stopped talking.

They reached the hotel she had requested and she paid the fare, including a tip that was not stingy but also not so large that he would remember it. Declining his offer of assistance, she got out of the taxi and watched it drive away. Once it was out of sight, she picked up her bag and started walking. Four blocks away she went into another hotel and checked in.

The police questioned all the taxi drivers who had been at LAX in a three-hour period after flight 471 had landed and showed them the composite sketch. None of them recalled seeing a flight attendant with a baby, and none of them recalled seeing a woman who looked anything like the one in the sketch.

Several people with children had taken taxis, but again, no driver recalled a two-month-old baby girl. Detectives Berryman and Roberts were just about out of ideas when they were visited by taxi driver Bob Cooper.

He wasn't sure if it meant anything, Cooper said, but he'd had a fare around the time the baby got snatched. The woman in his cab wasn't a flight attendant, though, and she had short blond hair and didn't wear glasses. Besides, the baby she had was a boy, and four months old at that. But he thought the cops should know about it anyway.

What had the baby looked like, Berryman asked, and Cooper described the child as best he could, considering that he hadn't gotten a real good look and had seen him only in the mirror. But the kid did have dark skin, and seemed small for his age, Cooper said.

Berryman showed Cooper the photo of Rachel that Denise had given him.

"Yeah, that kinda looks like the kid," Cooper said. "The coloring is right. And I did get a good enough look to see that it was a real pretty baby. But like I told the lady, what do I know about babies?"

Berryman took a gamble and called in the police artist. Taking the composite sketch of the woman called Alice Metliff, they altered it, changing the hair and taking away the glasses.

"That's her!" Cooper exclaimed. "Gee, I guess I done okay, huh, guys?"

He had done more than okay, they assured him, and started immediately for the hotel he'd left her at, hoping that by the end of the day they would be returning Denise Ryland's baby to her.

The desk clerk at the hotel was shown the sketch, but didn't recognize the woman. Nevertheless, the police performed a thorough room-to-room search. There was no sign of the woman. Discouraged, they canvassed the area and checked other nearby hotels. They came up empty, and again it seemed as though the kidnapper and baby had vanished into thin air.

Meanwhile, halfway across the country, a security guard at the Clairborne Hotel near O'Hare Airport entered a room whose door had had a "Do not Disturb" tag on it all day long, thus arousing the suspicions of the housekeepers. To the security guard's shock he found a woman bound and gagged on the bed. After releasing the terrified young woman she told them a tale of a room service waitress who had come to her door with a complimentary basket of fruit and bottle of wine. She had drunk one glass of the wine and eaten a pear, and remembered nothing after that until she had awakened tied hand and foot. The young woman, as it happened, was a flight attendant for West Lines Air. Her name was Cathy Thompson.

18

Jerry Ryland had regretted not being able accompany his wife and daughter to Los Angeles, but the Beaker Supermarkets presentation was crucial to the survival of his public relations agency. Ever since the merger of his company, Ryland Inc., with Montclair Communications, customers seemed uncertain about the new arrangement, and business had been slow and accounts were declining.

So far, Beaker, a medium-sized grocery store chain with eighteen stores in Chicagoland, had been loyal and stayed with him. A third generation, family-owned operation, they too were in a huge struggle with larger nationally-franchised discount grocery stores. In a bid to maintain their market share, the Beaker family had entrusted their ad business to the fledgling Ryland-Montclair Group.

Jerry had been in advertising and public relations ever since he had graduated from college, and had spent several years with a couple of the larger outfits in Chicago. But even then he had known his talents were better suited for a more personal environment, and with financial support from his wife, he had started and built the small but profitable company, which he had been running for five years.

Jerry was long on talent and was extremely creative, but the business and financial end of the business bored him—and besides, he wasn't very good at it either. He and Denise talked it over, and figured that having a partner would be a good idea. He had known Elena Montclair for some time, and she seemed to be a good fit as a partner. Her own agency was small, a sound and well-run business, and her business practices closely matched his own. With his creativity and contacts and her financial acumen, it seemed that they would make a winning team.

Unfortunately, after an initial few months of success, business began to taper off, and they lost a few key accounts. A number of larger agencies had begun cruising for some of the smaller agency accounts, eliminating competition and broadening their bases, and the Beaker Supermarkets account was the last major piece of business Ryland-Montclair had. If Beaker didn't go for this latest presentation, Ryland-Montclair could go under. Jerry was determined not to let that happen.

As usual, he tapped into his athletic experience to give him guidance. He remembered when Memphis State was down by six points in the Sugar Bowl during his junior year. The football team didn't have much of a loyal and supportive fan base, and every one of their athletic endeavors had always been considered second rate in the eyes of gridiron fanatics in the land of the mighty Southeastern Conference. As Alabama fans chanted, "Roll, Tide, Roll," the MSU fans sat glum, discouraged, and silent. Jerry Ryland, a strong but slow halfback from southern California, took the ball on a draw play up the middle. With less than two minutes to go, a perfectly executed block by wiry wide-out Jarvis Greer gave him a sliver of daylight, and Jerry ran sixty-five yards for the winning touchdown. Memphis State won that Sugar Bowl because Jerry Ryland didn't give up. True to character, he wasn't about to give up now.

He had put more into this presentation than any he had ever done before. The billing for the Beaker account represented forty percent of Ryland-Montclair's anticipated income for the year. Side by side, Jerry and Elena had worked tirelessly on the presentation. No expense had been spared in their effort to hold onto the account; costly storyboards were commissioned and a videotape of a possible television commercial was made. Probably the most radical part of their proposal was a pitch to redesign the stores. From first-hand experience, Jerry knew all too well how difficult it was for working couples to find the time in their busy schedules to plan and prepare balanced meals, something that was even more important when the couples had children. Jerry planned to present to Beaker an idea for a full gourmet deli in each store that offered hot, nutritious, ready-to-serve meals, and then base the advertising campaign on the convenience of healthy food-to-go.

In a conference room at Beaker's home office, Jerry and Elena made their pitch. They had done extensive market research and Jerry was sure that his idea mill had ground out the best material he'd ever done. He did his best work when the heat was on, and the pressure energized him. For her part, Elena had made sure that the tables balanced and the spreadsheets clicked.

The presentation was well-received; however, it soon became obvious that Jonathan Beaker, the son of the store's founder and chief financial officer, was lukewarm to the proposal. It would be very expensive to redesign the stores he said, frowning. At that point Elena turned on her charm. The only female in the room, she explained in detail how Jerry's creative approach to his stores and their products would appeal to women. Knowing that women were the primary shoppers for most families, the younger Beaker listened attentively to what she had to say.

She emphasized the hectic schedules of two-career families, and how Beaker Supermarkets could relieve some of the pressure on full-time working women and too-busy-to-cook soccer moms. Adding upscale entrees in smaller portions for singles, she added, would be a fresher and more attractive alternative to frozen dinners and fast food.

Elena's presentation was the final stroke in convincing Jonathan Beaker to give his okay. As the meeting concluded and the contract was signed, Jerry maintained his calm and professional demeanor, but his mind was flashing dollar signs: Not only had they preserved the Beaker account by increasing the billing for the next three years, they could also offset their losses from other lost accounts. Besides, the success of the Beaker campaign would bring new accounts and help the business grow again.

As they left Beaker headquarters, Jerry and Elena were ecstatic.

Jerry couldn't wait to talk to Denise and give her the news. He thought of calling her on her cell phone, but she was traveling with the baby, so he decided to try to reach her later at his mother's place.

Meanwhile, Jerry and Elena celebrated their victory by going out to dinner at the Dessert Company, and afterward to one of Chicago's trendy new cigar bars. Over brandy and a couple of vintage Macanudos they toasted the future like soul mates joined by mutual talent and shared success, discussing the Beaker campaign and planning the pursuit of other accounts.

Elena was a beautiful woman. She was not much over five feet tall, but still she had a commanding presence. With a rich mahogany complexion, beautiful brown eyes, and an hourglass figure, she was as physically different from Denise as day from night. Jerry and Elena had clicked instantly and got along very well, but other than long days and a few late nights at the office, they hadn't spent much time together and their relationship was strictly business.

As the evening progressed, Elena had a few drinks too many, and by the time they left the bar she was giddy and disoriented. Jerry, not in much better shape himself, was nevertheless better able to navigate, so he decided to drive her home. As he walked her to her door, her fragrance teased his senses, and found her even more intoxicating than the brandy he had drunk.

"You really saved that meeting today," Jerry said as she fumbled with her key. "I thought for sure we'd lost them until you stepped in with that stuff on single-servings of pot roast and meatloaf."

"You know, Jerry, a lot of guys would be too intimidated to let a woman participate in a presentation that important—even when she's a partner," she answered. "That's why I wanted to go into business with you. You treat me as a full equal."

"You've made your own way in this town, Elena. I'd never treat you as anything but my partner, a full partner in every way. Besides, I care about you."

She waggled a finger at him. "Now, what would Denise think about that?" she said with a mischievous grin.

"Lucky for us, Denise isn't here," he answered just as mischievously. He shook his head, wondering where that had come from.

His speech and his judgment were more than a little impaired by the brandy, and their teasing banter had aroused him beyond professional limits. He took Elena in his arms and kissed her. Unable and unwilling to say no, she responded passionately, pulling him into her apartment.

"Wait . . . wait a minute," he said as she closed the door behind them. "Are you sure you want to do this?"

She silenced his protests with another passionate kiss.

"What do you think?" she murmured.

She stumbled as she kicked off her shoes, and fell into Jerry's arms again.

"You're not afraid of me are you?" she asked, her arms still twined around his neck. Her breath was warm and sweet on his cheek.

"Should I be?" he asked.

Taking his hand, she led him to her bedroom. Meanwhile, at the Ryland home the phone rang and rang, echoing in the empty house.

19

The woman who called herself Alice Metliff spent just two hours in the hotel in Los Angeles. She needed only enough time to feed the child and be sure the baby was recovering from the drug. The woman jumped every time she heard a noise in the hallway, fearing that perhaps the police had tracked her down.

"Follow the plan!" she said to herself as she forced herself to be calm. Finally, it was time to move. She changed her clothes once more and ditched the blond wig, this time donning a wig with wavy black hair. Satisfied that her appearance now would draw less attention in comparison with the baby's, she picked up her bag and the baby, took the stairs to the first floor of the hotel, and, making sure that no one was nearby, slipped out a side door. As she walked down the street, she tried to blend with her surroundings, walking briskly with her head slightly down. The baby still slept most of the time; even though she had been given only a small amount of the sedative on the plane, it would probably take a few more hours to totally wear off.

The woman proceeded along the sidewalk to the rear of the Fun '50s Diner, where she was told the car would be. Sure enough, there was a black Ford Escort with the keys inside. Inside the trunk were fresh clothes, a car seat, and a bag of necessities for the baby, including two canisters of formula. There were also plane tickets for her and the baby.

Anxious to get out of Los Angeles as soon as possible, she got in the car and drove south to Long Beach. She concentrated on her driving; she couldn't afford to have a cop stop her for speeding or running a stop sign now.

In Rossmoor, just south of where Highway 605 meets the 405, she pulled off the road. She changed to another car, then took the 405 south to El Toro. There, she took I-5 south to San Diego, finally arriving at San Diego International Airport.

She had done her job. She had earned what was rightfully hers. All she had to do now was fly back to Chicago.

20

July 1999
San Diego, California

"Today will be a clear crisp day with a strong ocean breeze this morning. A cold front is moving onshore and we'll notice the change. Expect a few clouds this morning and a high temperature near seventy degrees. Highs will range in the sixties in the foothills, and we'll have a chance of rain in the mountains with temperatures in the middle forties."

—Joe Lizura, the golden-haired KNSD-TV meteorologist with the surfer-boy looks.

Six hours had passed since the plane carrying Denise Ryland and her baby had landed. The airport had been turned upside-down on the slim chance that the baby would be found, or the kidnapper would still be there hiding with the baby. By now, a city-wide all-points bulletin was out, and no fewer than one hundred officers were looking for baby Rachel and the woman who had taken her. News broadcasts about the tragic event had already aired on all the local stations.

Forensic experts had gone over the flight attendant's serving station and the airplane exit door, turning up clear fingerprints on both areas for the new and now missing flight attendant. Unfortunately, the owner of the prints had no prior police record, but other leads had panned out, and so far the flight attendant who called herself Alice Metliff was now the primary suspect.

From a live remote at the airport, KNSD-TV news anchor Alan Frio updated viewers. "Still not much new on the breaking news this evening from Los Angeles International Airport regarding the infant missing from flight 471 from Chicago," he said. "Information we have so far indicates that when the flight landed in Los Angeles earlier today, a young mother apparently was unable to locate her two-month old baby. A city-wide hunt is underway for a woman who allegedly posed as a flight attendant and who presumably took the child. This is the first kidnapping in the airport's history. We'll keep you posted on this bizarre story as details unfold. Back to you in the studio."

In a one-story fifties-era hotel room near San Diego International Airport, the woman calling herself Alice Metliff was eating a greasy cheeseburger and fries and watching TV. Suddenly, the news report about the missing baby came on. Panicked, she nervously placed a call to Chicago.

The call was not well-received. Instead of praise for a job well done so far, she was berated instead. The last thing she needed in her current frame of mind was a tongue lashing, and the yelling, screaming, and insults coming from the other end of the phone only upset her more. The last remark from her contact chilled her blood.

"If you make even the slightest mistake, or vary from the plan one more time—I swear, you stupid moron, I'll turn you in to the police. I'll disappear, and you'll rot in jail." She began to protest but there was nothing but the dial tone.

The woman sat and sulked for a while. He had called her stupid, and she hated being called stupid. She was frightened by the news bulletin, or she wouldn't have called him. But he had specifically told her not to call him—ever—so maybe it was understandable that he was so angry.

Besides, this wasn't the first time she had strayed from the plan. She cursed her independence. After all, she'd been given a job to do, and everything had been arranged, down to the finest detail. All she had to do was follow orders.

But she hated being ordered around, even when the scheme was going to pay off so richly. Her anger grew at the thought of being treated as nothing more than a flunky, especially when she was doing all the dangerous parts. She was a good actress; she knew it and they knew it too, so they should treat her better. Still, she knew she'd better not to make any more mistakes, or they might not pay her—or worse.

She picked up the remote and flipped through the stations to see what else about the kidnapping might be on the news. Finally, another report came on the NBC affiliate, this one showing a police artist's renderings of the alleged kidnapper. The woman looked in the mirror and was relieved to see that with the different wig, she now bore almost no resemblance to the sketched images shown on TV.

Denise frantically continued trying to reach Jerry, and was frustrated to reach only the answering service or their answering machine at home. She called his cell phone number several times, but only got the message that "the party is not available." Jerry was notorious for forgetting to keep his cell phone charged, and Denise's agitation mounted. *Where could he be?* she wondered.

She had realized early on she'd have to tell Jerry's family about the baby's disappearance before they saw it on the news, and with a sick feeling, she'd picked up the phone to call his mother.

Jerry's father had died less than two years ago; the couple had been married for thirty-five years, and Althea Ryland was still grieving from the loss. But when Denise told her and Jerry's sister, Monica, the horrible news, their concern was for her, and they insisted she leave the airport hotel and come home with them. She willingly agreed, feeling the need to have family around her. She notified the police of where she could be reached, and Althea and Monica whisked her to their home; as the hours dragged by they took turns trying to reach Jerry.

In vain, she tried to send her thoughts over the two thousand miles to him. *Where are you, boyfriend? I need you.*

It was now approaching eight o'clock. The police had reported the discovery of the bag containing the flight attendant's uniform and glasses in the trash at the airport. Combined with their knowledge of her using a disguise, they knew she would likely continue to change her appearance, so they would have to focus on looking for women with young babies. They promised they would keep her updated as the investigation proceeded.

"Denise, you need to lie down and get some rest," Monica Ryland told her that evening. "The police are going to find Rachel, and I'll wake you when they call."

"No," Denise answered her. "I can't sleep, I can't even sit still. Besides, I need to get hold of Jerry." She held the pink blanket and bunny that had been in Rachel's carrier, unable to bring herself let go of them for even a moment. She then looked at Monica in anguish.

"Oh, Monica, I've been so . . . Your wedding—this has ruined everything . . ."

Monica wrapped her arms around Denise and rocked her.

"Don't you even think about that, honey," she soothed. "The most important thing right now is to get Rachel back."

They talked for a while longer, then Denise went into the living room where Althea Ryland sat alone staring out the window at the gathering twilight. Denise sat down beside her, and the older woman sighed and took her hand.

"I thought I'd had enough pain when my husband died," she said. "But this . . . I don't know if I can take this . . . We were all going to be together as a family again."

Tears ran down Denise's face, and she shook her head. "Rachel's probably wet. Whoever took her left her baby bag and diapers. I fed her on the plane—that was so long ago!—she's hungry now. And her bunny . . . she won't be able to sleep without it . . ." A sob caught in her throat.

"There, now," Althea said, putting her arm around her daughter-in-law. "Whoever took her will take care of her, be sure she's fed."

"If its money they want, we can raise a couple hundred thousand. If we sell Jerry's business, we can probably raise a little more. And I still hold stock with Fisk and Ryan, and we could sell that . . ." Denise rambled.

Monica came in and joined them. "That's right," she said. "We'll give them what they want, and they'll give her back. We just need to wait."

Still leaning against Althea's shoulder, soothed by the comforting arm around her, Denise dozed.

She awoke with a start to find herself stretched out on the couch with a light blanket over her. It was dark outside. Shaking the grogginess from her head, she looked at her watch. It was almost eleven-thirty. It would be nine-thirty in Chicago—Jerry surely must be home by now. She reached for the phone on the end table and again tried to call him.

From her legal experience, she knew that in the majority of child kidnappings one of the parents was involved. The police had questioned her about that, but she and Jerry were not having any problems, so that was not an issue.

But as the answering machine at their home picked up again, worry and doubt began to grow. Where in the world was he when she needed him so? She hung up and almost jumped out of her skin when the phone rang even before she had taken her hand off it.

"Jerry? Where have you been?" she cried. Disappointed, she heard Detective Kyle Berryman on the other end.

He had nothing new to report, but wanted to let her know they were busy following up on potential leads she had given them earlier in the day.

"We checked on LaVergne Hinson Brystadt," he said. "She's been a busy little bee, visiting her brother on Death Row a lot, helping him ready his appeal, and raising funds for a new lawyer. But we haven't located her as yet."

"How about Linda Richards?" Denise asked. She ran her hand over the pink blanket as it lay on her lap, smoothing it out. Monica came into the room, her face falling as Denise shook her head.

"Richards' interior design class ended last week," Berryman said. "According to her roommate, right now she's in Florida on vacation. We're doing a search of hotels in the Fort Lauderdale area."

"It must be one of those two," Denise said. "I can't believe Tucker Boatman would be involved. He's already had enough trouble. Anything else would destroy his wife; she's fragile."

"We checked on them anyway. As far as whe can tell, they're at home going about their business. By the way," he continued. "Your private detective friend has been dropping by, keeping tabs on them."

"Romanski? Bless his heart!" Denise said.

She hung up and curled up on the couch on her side. The thought that her baby might never come home, becoming just another face on the side of a milk carton, was something Denise could not bear. In the darkness, clutching the pink blanket and bunny in her arms, she cried herself to sleep.

21

July 1999
Chicago

"Today will be a lovely day in Chicago. The cold front that moved through yesterday has left some cooler, drier air in place, so the normally oppressive summer humidity will not be with us today. Highs will be near seventy along the lake, and will range in the mid-seventies farther inland. After the insufferable heat wave we had last summer, this is quite refreshing."

—NBC 5 meteorologist Byron Miranda,
reporting on location from Garfield Park.

The next morning, his head pounding and regret filling his heart, Jerry Ryland went home. He stumbled in the door, tossed his jacket on the floor, and went right to the refrigerator for something other than alcohol to drink. He pulled out the milk and, not bothering with a glass, took a gulp right from the carton. As he shut the refrigerator door he spied Denise's note, secured by a little squirrel-shaped refrigerator magnet:

We miss you and can't wait until you get to L.A.
Love, Rachel and Mommy

Jerry felt ill. He realized how much he had to lose. How could he have risked destroying his family? He had never been a philanderer; of course, he'd had his share of flings in college, just wild-oats stuff—a couple of cheerleaders, the drum majorette. There also had been that little girl who had tutored him in chemistry—what was her name? He couldn't remember—a timid little chick he probably had led on a bit more than he should have. But from the time he met Denise, she'd been the only one for him. Vowing that nothing like the episode of the night before would ever happen again, he uttered a silent prayer of thanks that he and Elena had both been so drunk that once they hit the bed they had decided to get "just a little rest." They had fallen asleep before anything truly regrettable took place.

Even though he hadn't followed through with actually cheating on his wife, deep inside he knew he still was guilty of betraying her. Still bleary-eyed as he walked through the bedroom heading for the shower, he didn't notice the blinking red light on the answering machine. Later, as he drove to work, he thought of calling Denise in California. He checked the time; it was only five A.M. on the West coast, so he decided to wait for a few hours.

Jerry was pretty sure that Denise would be irritated that he hadn't called the evening before, and he wondered how he'd explain it to her. He decided he'd just say that he'd had a few drinks too many celebrating the Beaker presentation, and was too drunk to drive, so he fell asleep at the office. There had been many times in the past when she had been the one whose work had kept her away with late nights at the office, so she would understand.

But when Jerry got to his office, Elena was already there, her expression deeply serious. "Thank God you're here," she said. "Sit down, I have something to tell you."

"Elena," he interrupted, "look—last night was a mistake. You're a wonderful woman, but I love my wife. What happened last night—"

"Yes, Jerry, it *was* a mistake; we were wrong," she agreed. "But there's something much more important going on. Jerry, you have to go to Los Angeles right away. Denise called. She's been trying to reach you for hours. Something has happened to the baby. Rachel is missing."

He sagged into the chair behind his desk, his mouth open. Surely he must have imagined what he had just heard. Elena told him about the frantic phone messages from California, and that perhaps one of Denise's former "victims" in a legal struggle might be involved in the kidnapping.

Agonized, he covered his face with his hands. "Hell! I was there in your apartment trying to get my groove on, while my daughter was— Oh, God—"

"Drop it, Jerry. Right now you just need to go. I've already reserved a seat for you on the next plane to L.A."

He looked at her gratefully. "Thank you, Elena," was all he could say as he stumbled to his feet and dashed out the door.

22

There had been a couple of close calls in the San Diego airport, when it seemed that security was watching too closely. But her reservations had been made well in advance and she came up to the flight at the very last minute, and the woman easily made it through the gate and onto the plane. Once they were in the air and on the way to Chicago, she was quite content. She held her prize in her arms, and everything now was going according to the plan.

She desperately needed to go to the restroom, but that was where Denise Ryland had made her first mistake, and she would not do the same. She decided to wait until the plane landed.

Her biggest problem was that for some reason she was having trouble keeping the child quiet. Rachel had awakened back in the motel in San Diego and had fussed most of the night. The woman had changed the baby's diaper several times, even though it was dry, and had tried rocking her and singing a lullaby, but nothing worked. Now on the plane she was crying hard and had been doing so for more than an hour. She had taken one of the bottles at the motel but the formula didn't seem sit to well on her stomach. The woman considered giving the child more of the drug she had dosed her with the day before, but decided against it for fear of perhaps killing her.

Fortunately, people had seemed sympathetic to her predicament and no one had confronted her about the crying child. The baby still wore the blue-striped sweater and cap, and the woman kept her swathed in the blue receiving blanket; aside from commenting on what a shame it was the "little guy" didn't seem to feel very well, nobody seemed to notice anything unusual.

Four hours later, after a long, noisy journey, they landed at

O'Hare. The woman got off the plane and went to the ladies room. She willed the baby to stop crying, but she wouldn't. As she walked through the airport, the televisions posted throughout the terminal showed a report about the California kidnapping of the child of a Chicago couple. The woman lowered her head and walked faster, careful to avoid the police who now seemed to be everywhere. Keeping her pace deliberate, she made her way toward the exit and the car that was waiting for her.

As she approached the door, she froze. She could not believe her eyes. For the second time in two days, she was encountering Jerry Ryland at the airport. Looking disheveled and in a hurry, he bolted toward the gate. Suddenly he stopped and looked around, as if searching for something in particular.

The baby continued to fuss. Was it possible Jerry recognized his daughter's cries? The woman didn't worry about him knowing her, but what would happen if he caught a glimpse of his own baby?

He was no more than fifteen feet from her. Unsure whether to move, she stood rooted to the spot and holding her breath for what seemed like an hour. Other travelers, annoyed by the woman with the screaming baby, rudely pushed past her and continued on through the door. Jerry, still seeming to sense something, turned in her direction and looked right at her, and she was now sure he would be attracted by the baby's crying. He was too distracted to notice, however, and soon he moved on, caught up in the kaleidoscope of the crowd. Almost weak with relief, she continued out the door.

A man stood outside near the taxi stand, glaring at her menacingly. Shaken by the sight of him, she hurried toward him.

He shoved her into the back seat. "Are you trying to get us caught? Shut that brat up!"

She knew better than to argue with him, so she stayed quiet all the way to the hotel where the exchange was to take place. Even though she had delivered as she was supposed to, she couldn't help feeling nervous. She knew that she had deviated from the plan once more, and sooner or later she would pay for it.

23

For Jerry Ryland this was probably the worst day of his life. In a twenty-four-hour period he had struggled to save his business, almost cheated on his wife, and his precious baby girl had been lost. He was completely out of breath when he arrived at the terminal.

Upon rushing into the airport, he heard a baby cry, stopping him in his tracks. His first thought was that Rachel had been found and she and Denise had come home. For a moment he looked excitedly around, but saw only two couples with toddlers and one woman with a small infant. That child was dressed in blue, though, and the woman was not Denise. Sadly, he rushed on to the ticket counter.

He breathlessly explained his dilemma to the clerk. "I have a reservation already, and I'm running a little late, but I've got to get on the flight to L.A.! My wife flew out yesterday and someone kidnapped our baby off the plane!"

"Oh, my God! I saw that story on the news!" the counter attendant replied and quickly printed his ticket and boarding pass. Jerry had fifteen minutes before the flight was scheduled to take off, and he took advantage of the extra time to call Denise at his mother's house.

When Denise heard his voice, she burst into tears. The fine thread of hope that she had been holding on to was wearing thin. She had always been very strong, and Jerry was alarmed to find her beginning to break.

"I'm so sorry, Jerry," she wept. "It was all my fault. I didn't leave her at all, except to go to the restroom, but she was there when I got back. But then I fell asleep and . . . I guess that's when they took her. Please forgive me."

"You're not to blame, and there's nothing to forgive," he told her. "I love you and we're going to find our baby and bring her home."

"I think I must have been given something that knocked me out. They drew some blood and are checking the glass I drank from, testing for drugs." She paused, gathering her thoughts.

"Jerry, the police are questioning my old clients. They think somebody is out to get even with me, somebody I litigated against," she said struggling to find answers. "After all, I stomped on a lot of toes pretty hard."

"Denise, try not to worry. Whoever took our baby will be caught, and they are going to have hell to pay."

Jerry ached for his wife as she poured her heart out. Teary-eyed himself, he apologized for not being there with her. Again, he assured her that he did not blame her for what happened. His flight was called, and he lovingly said his good-byes. With his head hung low, he boarded the plane. He tried to convince himself that there was still hope for finding their baby, but some of the victims who lay along the path of Denise's legal career were capable of deep hatred, and were grudge-filled, powerful, and capable of revenge. Even so, to steal a baby from its mother was a torture more searing than a blazing knife.

On the plane, he thought about the cyclone that tore apart his life in the past day. He debated whether to tell Denise about his drunken lapse with Elena the night before, and decided that it would have to wait at least until Rachel was found. Then maybe he would confess and hope for her forgiveness.

When Jerry's plane landed at LAX the Ryland women were waiting, frazzled and depleted, but clearly cheered by his arrival. His mom and sister hadn't looked this weary since his father died, and the Denise who fell into his arms was not the one who left Chicago the day before. Stripped of her spirit when her baby was taken, she was little more than a crumpled puppet. If someone had wanted to get even with her, they certainly were doing a good job of it.

Also waiting for him at the airport were detectives Berryman and Roberts. Taking Jerry to a private room, they apprised him of the situation, asking if he had any enemies, business or personal. He shook his head mutely.

While the police were interviewing Jerry, an urgent call came from Chicago. A woman fitting the general size and shape of the suspect had been spotted at O'Hare about four hours earlier. She had been noticed because she was carrying a small infant. Berryman and Roberts showed Jerry the composite sketch. He shook his head, uncertain.

"I saw a woman with a baby," he said, "but she—the woman—had dark hair, wavy." He frowned, then picked up a pen and scribbled around the face on the drawing.

"That's her!" he shouted as he leaped to his feet, knocking his chair over. "That *is* the woman I saw at O'Hare!" His voice was so loud that Denise burst into the room, alarmed. He pulled her to him and took her face in his hands. "Babe, I saw this woman and Rachel in Chicago. I'm sure of it!"

He turned then and slammed his fist against the wall. "I can't believe I let her get past me! I remember I looked at her because I heard the baby. It was crying with that hiccuping sound Rachel makes when she's unstrung. Damn!" Denise began to cry again. That he had been so close . . . The thought of a stranger transporting her child across the country was almost more than she could bear. Jerry held her and then sat her on the couch. He looked deep into her eyes as he wiped her tears away.

"We can't lose hope now," he tenderly told her. "We have to be strong for Rachel. Come on, babe, let's go get our baby."

24

The car carrying the kidnapper and the stolen baby arrived at the hotel amidst the screams of the baby and the curses of the driver. While she was happy that she had completed the first and riskiest part of her task, the woman knew that the most important part of this mission was still to come.

She got out of the car and the man drove away to park. She was relieved to be away from him for a while. Just being near him made her queasy. He was big and mean, with a badly scarred face and hate-filled eyes; everything about him indicated he was capable of unspeakable evil.

The kidnapper walked through the lobby and went directly to suite 1211. The door was open, and she walked in and closed it behind her. The light in the sitting room was dim but bright enough for her to see what she was after. The suitcase was on the bed, as she had been told it would be. She knew that she wasn't supposed to even touch it just yet, but it was so tempting. Besides, as she furtively looked around, she seemed to be alone in the room

She placed the baby at the head of the bed and opened the suitcase. Her eyes glittered, and for the first time since the ordeal began she found herself smiling. Inside the suitcase was her true prize—a half-million dollars.

"Finally! It was worth it after all," she said to herself.

As the woman gently and lovingly caressed the bills, she thought of all of the sacrifices she had made, and of her future as a wealthy woman. Out of the corner of her eye she glimpsed a dark figure moving toward her. She spun around and ducked but didn't move fast enough; and a vicious backhanded slap knocked her to the floor and she tasted her own blood. She had violated the plan again and this time she paid for it.

"I did everything the way I was supposed to," she whined. "I just wanted to see my money."

The fracas upset the already fussy Rachel and she howled.

"Get up and shut that kid up!" the man snarled as he violently kicked the woman in the ribs. "I'll be rid of you soon," he muttered as he filled a glass with the cheap scotch he drank.

"I'm sorry . . . I know I made some mistakes but I was afraid . . . and the baby won't stop crying!" She knew her life was on the line.

"Well, you'd better get her to stop, or else . . ." He held up his hand as if to strike her again, then he stomped into the next room and slammed the door.

The baby was still whimpering. The woman frantically wrung her hands, not knowing what to do. She had given the baby another bottle, but the child had thrown up most of it. The woman picked her up and paced the room with her.

"Soon *I'll* be rid of *him*," she muttered resentfully to herself as she gingerly touched her aching ribs.

She paced faster in her efforts to quiet the infant, but she only cried louder. As her wails intensified, another voice came from the other room.

This was a voice the woman knew well. It was the voice that had first described the plan to her. The woman had no idea who it belonged to, only that the person behind this voice had made a pact with her. Together they would punish their mutual enemy and make her pay, and each of them would have their respective prizes.

But now it was time to settle their business. The woman who called herself Alice had performed according to the agreement, and she handed the baby over. The voice immediately began to comfort the fussy baby, and mercifully she began to quiet down. The woman closed her eyes and sighed; the constant crying by the baby had been thoroughly annoying.

The awful man left to get the car, and the kidnapper and the voice now sat face-to-face in the dimly lit room, eying each suspiciously in the half light. So very sorry the man had lost patience and yelled at her over the phone, the voice apologized. She congratulated her on a job well-done. Please, the voice said, have some tea; relax, let's talk a while longer. The kidnapper kept glancing over at the briefcase full of money, eager to be on her way, but there was one more set of instructions. This had not been a part of the original bargain, but the woman who called herself Alice relished this new task. The voice had a soothing effect on her. After all, when she was upset because the uniform was too snug, the voice on the phone had calmed her fears. When she was fearful of being discovered while trying to pose as a flight attendant, or that she wouldn't be able to leave the plane unnoticed with the baby, the memory of the gentle voice and its instructions renewed her confidence.

To a great extent, she trusted the voice; it had usually been kind and supportive. The horrible man had treated her miserably, though; she would gladly carry out the last instruction the voice requested, and the woman smiled as she sipped her cup of hot tea. The extra half-million dollars the voice offered was a great incentive for undertaking this new phase of the plan. They finished their conversation, and the man came to take the kidnapper to complete the final task of their evil alliance.

25

"Babe, it's time to go. We have to get on the plane."

Jerry had his arm around Denise, gently urging her along.

"I can't," she replied, fear glazing her eyes.

"Denise, we have to. Rachel needs us. If we don't go now, we may never be able to find her."

She was terrified of getting on a plane again. It brought back memories of losing her baby. The trip to California replayed over and over in her mind. If only she hadn't gone to the restroom. What had she eaten and drunk? Why had she fallen asleep? Wrong. Everything she had done was wrong, and now her baby, the whole center of her world, was gone.

She tormented herself, thinking back to the three big cases she had participated in where people had been damaged beyond repair. "Why did I scorn the Hinsons in the Grandma Murders? Why did I go along with Daniel Richards' plan? What on earth possessed me to humiliate Tucker Boatman and his family?" No matter how she asked the questions, the answer was the same: It was her fault.

But she needed to be realistic now, to think clearly. It wasn't clear to either the police or to her that a person she'd wronged might have kidnapped Rachel. The Boatmans were under constant surveillance and had not left Chicago since the baby was taken. LaVergne Hinson Brystadt had been located at a religious retreat where she had gone to pray for her brother. According to Linda Richards' mother, Linda had spent the last few weeks having fun in the sun in the Bahamas with the new love of her life. It seemed that none of them could have kidnapped Rachel. So who? Who?

As Denise sat next to Jerry on the plane, she clutched the stuffed toy from the infant carrier in her arms. Her bond with her child had been reduced to the comfort of a small pink bunny.

She performed her own self-inquisition, unable to escape the blame. If only she had been half the person that her mother had been perhaps she wouldn't have enraged people who acted with such unconscionable behavior. Mama had been a teacher for thirty-six years and had also served on the school board before the car accident that claimed her life. Helen Beaumont had been a strong, proud woman, an honorable woman, and she had worked to instill those same qualities in her daughter, Denise.

Jerry wiped the tears from her face. "Stay strong, babe. Rachel needs you. *I* need you," he said. "We'll get her back—you have to believe that."

She squeezed his hand and lay her head on his shoulder.

"Do you remember when we were back in school?" he asked.

Thinking he was just trying to distract her, she nodded.

"Who are we?"

"What?"

"Who are we?" he asked again.

Puzzled, she thought for a moment. "The mighty, mighty Tigers?" she said hesitantly, her voice lacking conviction.

He nodded. "And how do we win?"

Now she understood. "We never give up," she replied, looking into his eyes.

It was what fans had shouted to give Memphis State a lift when they were behind on the scoreboard. After Jerry led his team to victory in the Sugar Bowl he had run to the student section and led them in that cheer. Jerry Ryland never gave up, and deep down inside, Denise knew Rachel's safe return depended on her not giving up either.

"Hang on, sweetie—Mommy and Daddy are coming," she said aloud and smiled for the first time since her child had been taken.

26

An alert airport security officer in Chicago had spotted the kidnapper. He wrote down the license plate of the late-model car that she had ridden away in, a rental that had been reported stolen, and now all Chicago area police departments, in conjunction with the FBI, were hot on the trail of the missing baby.

They traced the stolen car to the south side of town, to a hotel whose reputation was less than upright. The police converged on the scene and watched and waited. Finally, a couple emerged from the hotel and climbed into the stolen car, the man taking the driver's seat and the woman, carrying a large bag, getting into the back seat.

The sergeant in charge cautioned his team over the two-way radio. Often accused of overreaction and unjustified shootings, they were now taking a cautious approach. They couldn't afford to risk losing their lead on the baby, so they followed the car at a safe distance for a few miles as it headed north on the Dan Ryan.

The man driving the stolen car took the ramp heading west onto the Eisenhower and suddenly sped off. Realizing that they had been spotted, the police hit their flashing lights and sirens, embarking on a high-speed chase that would go on for more than twenty minutes at speeds sometimes exceeding more than a hundred miles per hour.

The driver wove in and out of traffic, proving to be a worthy adversary even for the Chicago PD. However, as more police cars became involved in the pursuit, the job of evading them became more difficult.

Despite being thrown around in the back seat as the car careened about, the woman who called herself Alice remained calm. She was relaxed, almost to the point of drowsiness, and she wondered if there had been something in the tea she'd drunk at the hotel. She didn't mind, though, because now she knew she wouldn't lose her cool when her opportunity came to inject the driver with the syringe she had been given by the voice. She had been assured that the drug would act fairly quickly, which would give her a chance to escape. All she had to do was wait for the man to stop or at least slow down so she could inject him and then jump from the car. The main problem was that the man kept glancing in the rearview mirror at her; she would have to be alert for the first opportunity to strike.

The woman looked forward to destroying this horrible man with an intensity that bordered on obsession. That in itself would be a reward. But when she had accomplished her task she could collect her real reward—money.

The last thing she suspected was a double-cross, and that neither she nor the driver would get a chance to finish their missions.

The woman who called herself Alice shook her head and rubbed her eyes, trying unsuccessfully to think clearly. She began to worry that if the police caught them, she wouldn't be able to give the awful man the poison. She couldn't wait for him to stop, and decided to inject him as soon as he took his eyes off the rearview mirror. The car went speeding up behind a semi, and as the driver swerved to get around it, she leaned forward and grabbed his shoulder, plunging the needle into the side of his neck. The man howled in pain and grabbed at the syringe, but was too late; the injected drug was already coursing through his bloodstream.

"You damn dirty bitch!" he bellowed. "I'm going to make you—"

His words were cut off as he saw the car heading toward an oil truck. He jerked the steering wheel sharply but overcorrected. Already in a stupor from the drug, he made one last effort to control the car before his eyes rolled back and he lost consciousness.

In the back seat of the car and in a daze herself, the kidnapper was vaguely aware of the car crashing through the guardrail. She tried to figure what had gone wrong. She hoped the car would slow to a stop so she could escape, but it flip-flopped down the embankment, tossing her about like a rag doll. Finally the car came to a stop and she lay there, blood in her eyes clouding her vision and the poison in her system numbing her judgment. She smelled gasoline and saw flames licking at the dashboard. As the fire crept toward her she knew she should try to get out of the car somehow. If only she weren't so sleepy . . .

My money, she thought. *I have to get my money—*

And then there was only the hiss of flames and the sound of far-off sirens. She never heard the deafening explosion.

27

As she cuddled the baby, the woman watched the news on the television in the seedy hotel room. News helicopters nosily hovered over the Eisenhower Expressway, broadcasting scenes of the devastating accident that, according to the reporter, had claimed at least two lives. Police had been chasing two suspects in the kidnapping of a baby, the reporter said, and had gone off the road, causing a fiery explosion. Inside the car were the bodies of a man and a woman, identities unknown. As far as they could tell, the missing baby had not been in the car.

She smiled. Her plan had worked to perfection. She not only had the baby, but all the money too. Getting rid of the two accomplices had been easier than she had anticipated. *Their own fault*, she mused, thankful they had been so greedy. Now she didn't have to worry about one of them being caught and giving the whole thing away. So neat, so simple. Now she could have the life she had always wanted.

The next morning she got up at five o'clock. She hummed a lullaby to the baby as she pulled on a pair of plastic gloves and moved around the three rooms in the shabby suite with a cleaning rag. It was important to be sure there were no fingerprints or anything that could give any evidence about either her or her now-flambéed partners.

She had to act quickly. Her first concern was for the baby. The child had hardly stopped crying since it had been delivered to her, and she barely ate or slept. That couldn't go on. A quick trip to a doctor to be sure the baby was all right, and then they could leave Chicago.

She hated large cities, and always had, with their traffic jams, crime, dirt, and congestion. She knew of a perfect place to raise the baby. Now that she had all the money for herself, she could create a fine new life for herself and her little angel.

She caught her breath as her heart leaped. This was *her* baby now! This was how it would be from now on, just her and *her* little girl, alone and happy together. She did a final pass around the suite, then, satisfied that she had cleaned every surface, packed her bags and gathered up the baby. Then she loaded everything into the car, carefully secured the infant into a carseat, and left the past behind.

28

Denise and Jerry were horrified when they learned of the car crash that had claimed the life of the kidnapping suspect. The police reassured them that a thorough search had been done of the entire area, in case Rachel had been in the car and thrown from it on impact. No baby was found. But with the kidnapper dead, they feared that the chances of locating their baby were diminished. Perhaps new leads would come once the kidnapper and her companion were identified.

The police set up surveillance equipment at the Ryland home and put a tap on their phone. The investigation was still operating on the assumption that the kidnapping was an act of revenge, and they were still examining Denise's past law cases for possible suspects, but they couldn't completely rule out that it was a kidnapping for ransom. If that were the case, there would be a ransom demand; if it were indeed revenge, the kidnapper might take satisfaction in calling just to torment them.

But as afternoon changed to night and then to morning, there was nothing, with the exception of one call from an individual who called himself Grant Parker and who cackled, wanting to know if she really wanted her baby back. It turned out to be only a crank call inspired by the publicity surrounding the case, and was traced to a derelict who had made the call from a pay phone and who made his residence in the parking garage by—where else?—Grant Park.

The Rylands anxiously continued to wait for the phone to ring or for a note to be delivered—anything to let them know their daughter was alive and well. Their lives had been reduced to a waiting game, hoping for word from the lunatic who had taken their baby. With nerves on edge they waited, but as the third day of their nightmare progressed, there was still no word from the kidnapper.

Sitting in the waiting room of the emergency medical clinic and crooning to the baby in her arms, the woman fought to maintain a calm demeanor and hide the nervousness and fear that ate at her.

She had filled out all the necessary forms—address, date of birth, whether the baby had any allergies, name of pediatrician—careful to record the false information that she had created weeks before. She wondered for a moment if a doctor really needed to see the baby at this point; after all, the child had finally been able to keep down a bottle of formula. It was better to be safe than sorry, though, and she decided to go ahead with the checkup.

After what seemed like hours of waiting, she was finally led into an examination room. Dr. Alan Resnick, the pediatrician at the clinic, introduced himself and turned to the baby. He removed the little bonnet and quickly glanced at the light-haired, fair-skinned woman, a touch of surprise on his face.

"I get that look a lot," the woman said with a nervous little laugh. "She looks like her father."

Resnick weighed the child and asked about her medical history, and the woman explained how her daughter had seemed to have a little tummy ache and hadn't been eating too well. They had been visiting relatives in Chicago, she explained, and before they headed back home to Minnesota she thought she should get little Sherry looked at. The doctor nodded and listened to the baby's breathing and heart with his stethoscope. He checked her mouth and throat, and peered into her eyes and ears with a small light. With a little frown, he checked her eyes again.

"What is it?" the woman asked. "She's all right isn't she? Except for the tummy ache, of course."

"Well, her throat is a little raw, probably from crying," he said. "But she does seem to be rather dehydrated, and that's probably from not being able to keep her formula down." Fortunately, as an emergency clinic, they had a few more treatment options than a standard doctor's office, and Resnick suggested infusing some fluids intravenously to help stabilize the baby. They could observe her for a while, he said, and if everything seemed okay, then the woman and baby could be on their way.

The woman was vexed, but to protest would arouse suspicion, so she agreed. A nurse was called in, and she and the doctor worked to get an IV started in the baby, who howled her protest at being stuck with the needle. Tears stung the woman's eyes at the infant's renewed crying; she hated to see her hurt. Dr. Resnick jotted down a few notes in the baby's chart, then with a promise to check back in a few minutes, left the room.

Out in the hallway, Resnick pulled the nurse aside. "There's something fishy about this situation," he said in low tones. "That baby's eyes aren't right."

"What do you mean? Do you think she's blind?"

"No, nothing like that. It's her pupils—they don't react to light like they should." He chewed his lip and thought for a moment. "It's as if she's been heavily sedated. I think that baby's been drugged, and that's what's causing the dehydration."

"What should we do?" the nurse asked.

"If that IV doesn't pull her around in about ten minutes, then we may be dealing with a potentially life-threatening situation. Besides, if that woman has drugged her baby once, what's to stop her from doing it again?"

A few minutes later he checked on the baby again, but this time, looking her directly in the eye, he asked the woman point-blank if she had given the child anything besides formula. Of course she hadn't, she insisted, demanding to know exactly what he was insinuating.

He had meant no offense, he assured her. However, he did think the infant required further observation, possibly for at least another hour, to be sure the dehydration and stomach upset were cleared up.

The woman was really nervous now, and no longer able to hide it. Every minute that passed increased her chances of getting caught, and her elaborate plan would have been for nothing. Feeling like a tiger trapped in a cage, she knew she had to get out of there, and soon.

Alarmed, Resnick saw the woman's agitation. He decided he needed to act right away and excused himself again. Out in the hallway he urgently beckoned to the nurse.

"That baby still isn't acting right, and the mother, or whatever she is, is getting really antsy," he said. "Go into my office, where you can't be heard, and call the police. Tell them the situation, that the baby has been drugged, and to get here fast. I'm not sure how much longer I can keep them here."

The woman had opened the door of the examination room a crack when the doctor left and overheard what he said to the nurse.

Damn! she thought to herself as her anger rose. *That damned stupid moron—if she wasn't already dead, I'd kill her myself!*

The kidnapper was supposed to have just wiped a little of the tranquilizer across the baby's lips, not feed it to her. Now because of the kidnapper's incompetence, she stood to lose everything.

Dehydration or not, she had to act fast. Taking great care to keep from hurting the baby and causing her to cry again, she expertly disconnected the IV and wrapped the blanket around the baby. From the medicine cabinet she took some drugs and Pedialyte—that would be good for the dehydration, she knew—and placed them in her bag. Peering into the hallway to be sure the coast was clear, the woman slipped out of the room to the back door of the clinic and left.

By the time the police arrived the woman was miles away, but they now had definitive evidence that the baby was still in the Chicago area. They were able to get a full description of the woman from the doctor and nurse, and the clinic's security cameras had captured the woman and baby on film.

An all-points bulletin was sent out to the entire Chicago area police, and the description and stills of the video were distributed to the media. Unknown to her, most of the Chicago area was now aware of what she looked like. It seemed now that the woman would no longer be able to avoid detection and eventual capture. She had spent months planning and stalking Denise Ryland, but now the tables had turned, and it was she who had become the hunted.

She had been so careful, following her plan to the letter. She wished she hadn't had to take the baby to a doctor; that could have caused problems. But what choice had she had? Any mother would have done the same thing, and after all, she *was* the baby's mother now; it had been the right thing to do.

Anger at the kidnapper welled up in her again. This mess was all her fault, damn her. No wonder her precious baby cried almost nonstop. It was a miracle the idiot hadn't killed her.

She glanced in the rearview mirror at the baby, who continued to fuss. Deciding she couldn't let her go on like that, the woman turned onto a side road and drove until she found a secluded spot. There, she pulled over, turned off the ignition, and dumped the items she had taken from the clinic onto her lap. She filled a baby bottle with some of the Pedialyte, took the baby from the car seat, and coaxed her into drinking the liquid.

Nothing like this would ever happen again to this baby, she vowed as she held the infant close. She would shelter and protect her child from the rest of the world. Having her baby made her feel like the happiest woman in the world.

After the baby drank a few ounces of the Pedialyte, the woman held her against her shoulder and patted her back. A large burp reassured her, and she felt that everything would be all right now.

She berated herself for sending such a bumbling lame-brain to get the child instead of going herself. But she had always been afraid of flying and would never have been able to even board the plane, much less carry out the rest of the plan. In fact, it seemed that she had spent most of her life being afraid of almost everything. What she feared most was being alone; but now she had the baby, and she would never be alone again. She smiled and hummed a lullaby as her little darling drifted into a peaceful sleep. A big city like Chicago was no place to raise a child, the woman knew. They would live out in the country, and there she could raise her child in the slow-moving environment of a small town, the same one in which she'd grown up.

29

Denise and Jerry Ryland were elated when the police informed them that Rachel had been positively identified at the emergency clinic. Like a starving woman, Denise's eyes devoured the still photos taken from the clinic's security camera, leaving her giddy with relief at having tangible evidence that her baby was alive. By taking Rachel to a doctor, Denise felt that the kidnapper apparently was conscientious enough to be sure that the baby was well taken care of. The police kept to themselves the matter that the child had apparently been heavily drugged.

Denise and Jerry studied blowups of the security camera pictures of the woman, but neither of them recognized the face. For a flash, Denise thought there was something familiar about the woman, but she wasn't sure. She racked her brain, thinking about all the people she'd angered in court and trying to conjure their faces, but none of them matched the person in the photos.

The FBI had put together a profile on the suspect, and as the Rylands held onto each other for strength, they were carefully briefed on the situation. By now, the police explained, they believed that anyone who would protect the baby and care for the baby as her own was probably suffering from something called "surrogate mother syndrome"—the odd and frightening desire to steal a child to raise as one's own. If that was the case, and the suspect wasn't found soon, baby Rachel could disappear into anonymity and never come home to her parents. Denise looked at Jerry with naked terror in her eyes. Swallowing his own fears, he held his wife close.

"Remember, babe," he said. "We're the mighty, mighty Tigers—we never give up."

FBI agents and detectives from Chicago PD came to the Ryland home to give Denise and Jerry an update on the investigation. Confirmation that Denise's former law practice was related to Rachel's disappearance came when the bodies found in the burned automobile were finally identified through dental records. As they had feared, the baby snatching apparently was a crime of revenge.

The crash victims, however, had been involved in cases that were totally unrelated. One of them was Tucker Boatman, the stepfather of the young girl who had committed suicide at Newville High. The female was Linda Richards, the former wife of noted local attorney Daniel Richards.

The FBI surmised that Tucker Boatman had acted out of rage over the loss of his stepdaughter, and that he was most likely working for Linda Richards, whose well-to-do connections apparently had enabled her to finance the operation. Boatman had had several scrapes with the law, but he was hardly a criminal mastermind. His past history indicated that he was not a planner but a follower.

It had now been proven that Linda Richards had been the one impersonating a flight attendant and who had taken the baby from the plane. Denise had never actually met the woman face-to-face; she had seen only the incriminating photos from the divorce case, and most of those didn't leave clear impressions. Furthermore, Linda Richards had gained almost thirty pounds, changed her hair color, and worn glasses, so it was no wonder that Denise hadn't recognized her on the plane.

Linda had hated Denise intensely, holding her directly responsible for her humiliating divorce settlement, and she had made numerous phone calls to Denise over the past year, threatening to settle the score.

As this information sank in, Denise's sadness was replaced by anger. No half-baked bitch on a vengeance trip was going to tear her family apart, she determined, now defiant and ready to wield her meat axe as she went into battle for her child. A fresh storm was brewing—Hurricane Denise Ryland was back.

As the FBI agents talked, Denise took detailed notes, and when they and the detectives left she reached for her cell phone. She knew exactly who to call.

"Dale, I need your help," she said when Romanski answered the phone.

"I'm way ahead of you," he interrupted. "The Boatman woman has your baby."

"Tucker Boatman's wife—Cheryl's mother? How do you know?"

"I've been working on it ever since the news hit the airwaves from L.A.," he said.

"Look," she said. "I'll pay anything—do anything—to get Rachel back. And I mean *anything!* I don't care what happens to the woman."

"It may not be real easy, so you better listen to me. I'm going to tell you everything I've found out, and it's not pretty," Romanski said flatly. "Everything I know, the FBI and Chicago PD probably know, but they won't tell you," he added.

He told Denise about the background check he'd done on Jeanine Boatman. She had no known relatives; her last family member had been her recently deceased husband. She had quit her job as a registered nurse, becoming a recluse since her daughter's suicide the year before. However, about three months ago she had begun work as a pharmacist's assistant. She quit there suddenly last week, and after she left the pharmacy, it was discovered that several tablets and capsules of narcotics—phenobarbital, hyoscyamine, and Seconal—were missing. It was pretty certain that Jeanine Boatman had taken the drugs.

"Linda Richards must have slipped you some of the Seconal on the plane—trace elements of it were found in one of the glasses from there," Romanski told Denise.

Of course! She had thought the water with the lemon had tasted odd. No wonder she had slept so soundly. Fresh rage surged through her when she realized that Rachel must have been drugged too, to keep her from crying.

Dale Romanski continued his report. A routine check of Jeanine Boatman's bank records indicated that her late husband had recently closed their checking and savings accounts. Romanski figured that with those funds, along with the money from the cash settlement of the Newville School Board lawsuit received just six months ago, Jeanine Boatman was traveling with well over a million dollars in cash. Because she had no family or close friends, it was anyone's guess where she might be headed. However, with that much money, it was possible for her to go anywhere.

"I don't believe it. This is too much," Denise said, her voice edged with anxiety.

"You gotta hang on, kiddo," Romanski said. "You know I wouldn't have told you all this if I didn't think you could handle it."

She assured him that she was fine. "You're right. I can do this—I *will* do this! Just help me find my baby, please," she said.

"I will. I know your home phone is tapped and we don't want to tie it up, so keep your cell phone switched on. I'll be in touch."

For the first time since the ordeal began, Denise began to feel real hope. She knew she could depend on Dale Romanski to come through for her; he had never let her down before, and she was confident that he wouldn't now. More than any other man except her husband, she trusted Romanski, and she knew that he would use any means necessary to help reunite her with her baby.

That Jeanine Boatman was the primary suspect was something Denise found horribly disturbing. Denise herself had felt responsible for Cheryl Boatman's suicide, and could only imagine the level of blame the girl's mother assigned her. Denise was sure that the grief she felt when she miscarried her first child paled in comparison to what Jeanine Boatman had endured. And since Rachel's disappearance, Denise also had come to know how grief, when turned into anger, could definitely become hatred.

Jeanine Boatman had every reason to hate Denise. A brief wave of panic stabbed through her as she contemplated what that hatred might cause the woman to do. What if she harmed Rachel? What if—? No, she couldn't allow herself to think like that. She had to stay strong. If Jeanine intended to harm Rachel, she wouldn't have taken her to a doctor.

Denise's head was pounding, and she went into the bathroom for some aspirin, then gazed at the reflection in the medicine cabinet mirror. The face looking back at her was haggard and ashen, with dark circles around the eyes. A little voice nagged at her from the back of her mind. *Cut it any way you wish*, the little voice said, *you're to blame for all of this*. She shut her eyes tightly against fresh tears and asked herself how she could be such a loser.

Downstairs in the basement Jerry ran on his treadmill, as if he could somehow escape the blame he put on himself for the nightmare in which he and Denise were living. Compounding his agony was the guilt he felt for his weak moment with Elena. Jerry had had a strong Catholic upbringing, but he had never considered himself to be a particularly religious person. As sweat mingled with the tears on his face, he prayed for forgiveness and mercy, begging God for another chance to be a father to his little girl.

30

Jeanine Boatman was afraid the nosy doctor at the clinic might have called the police, so after leaving there she had driven on back roads for a while. Now she got on the Tri-State Tollway, handed her money to the clerk at the tollbooth, and headed north toward Wisconsin. She was happily taking her baby to their new home where life would be perfect, and she was blissfully unaware of the widening degree of manpower and technology being deployed to find them.

Actually, Jeanine was blissfully unaware of almost everything. All that mattered was that she now had a baby to replace the one she lost. The urge to get and keep a baby had begun after Cheryl's death, a longing that turned into a craving, a need that had grown into an uncontrollable and all-consuming animal lust.

Her picture and that of the baby had been circulated all through Illinois, Michigan, Indiana, and Wisconsin. As a result, the tollbooth clerk recognized her and flagged down a nearby state trooper who immediately began trailing her at a discreet distance. The trooper notified Chicago PD, who in turn notified the FBI, and they joined in the chase.

Dale Romanski was not far behind.

Jeanine headed north, enjoying the beautiful summer afternoon and bright sunny sky. It was a perfect day to start a new life. She longed to pull off somewhere, check into a motel, and get a little rest. She had forgotten how much energy a little baby took; the day-long crying and restlessness had worn her out. She didn't dare stop, though, for fear of the trouble the damned nosy doctor may have stirred up. At least her little darling had kept the Pedialyte down and had even managed to take a little formula, but she still was fussy.

As they drove past O'Hare, Jeanine couldn't help but smile at the irony. She had a morbid fear of flying, yet her baby, her new life, had come to her from an airplane.

Everything that was happening now was ironic, and sometimes confusing. She was glad that she hadn't had to manage the past several months alone, that she'd had her companions to advise her. It was they who had suggested that she contact that ridiculous woman, the bimbo divorcee who took all those crazy college courses and thought she was a sexpot but who actually looked like a grotesque, overaged, overweight Playboy bunny.

Jeanine's companions had also helped her construct the perfect plan, step by step. It had hurt to use the money from Cheryl's death, but it had come in handy when she had to bribe the flight attendant who had been recently fired from West Lines Air. He told her every detail of a flight attendant's duties and helped her get the fake ID for the fat, stupid bunny. But she hadn't needed her companions for everything. The drugs she knew how to get and use herself.

She continued north through Park Ridge and Des Plaines. She was less than two hours away from her destination, the small town where she had spent the happiest days of her childhood. She couldn't wait to get there. She had lived there with her maternal grandparents who had taken her in after the illnesses that had claimed her parents' lives. She remembered riding ponies in the meadow in the summer and sledding in the snow in winter. She remembered sunny days and picnics under the big old oak tree. Most of all, she remembered the cool water of the glacial spring-fed lake.

It was her favorite place in the world, and she had even gone there on her honeymoon—the second time she was married, not the first, not that any time spent in the company of Tucker Boatman could have been called a honeymoon. Nevertheless, she always had the fondest memories of her time at the lake. She couldn't wait to take the baby to the Venetian festival and see the excitement in her eyes as she watched the parade of boats light up the lake. She would show her the mail boat and the huge estates once owned by the most powerful families of Chicago. Lake Geneva, Wisconsin, would make a happy home for her new baby girl.

Jeanine was pulled from her reverie when the baby started to fuss again. She knew she would have to stop before too much longer.

"Mommy's gonna stop soon now, honey," she said to the baby as she pulled onto the exit ramp. "Then Mommy's gonna feed her sweet baby and give her some medicine to make her feel better."

She was a mommy again! The thought alone thrilled her. There were so many things she had wanted to do with her firstborn child that she hadn't been able to do. Roger Parkhill, Cheryl's biological father, and then Tucker Boatman, had never let her do anything. Tucker had at least treated her and Cheryl well, and in his own way, he probably really loved both of them. Maybe she should have cared more for Tucker, but any feelings she'd had for him had died when Cheryl did. He had changed after that, and become abusive and threatening. But now he was gone, and she could drive up to Door County and show the baby the lighthouses, with their booming foghorns and different colored lights, any time she wanted. "The Door" was another place she loved dearly, and going there was another experience she eagerly looked forward to sharing with her new child. She would do much better this time, she vowed, and she would be the best mother ever.

It was so good not having a man to complicate things. Looking back, she probably shouldn't have married either one of her husbands, but the companions had urged her to do so. Sometimes the companions didn't give good advice, and she became angry with them for that. The companions, tiny voices that only she could hear, that over the years had grown louder and more insistent, had started talking to her when she was in college, when she had felt odd, different—a

Northern girl thrust into a strange Southern atmosphere, sad, lonely, always haunted by the loss of her parents. It was then her companions would visit her, at first infrequently, as she sat alone in her dorm room or walked along a lonely trail on the campus ground at night. She found them disturbing, wondering if they were angels or devils.

Then she had met *him*, and the days on campus with him were wonderful and the nights were full of magic, and the companions stayed away for a while, hurt and angry, probably. But then he left her and they came back, whispering, whispering to her, keeping her company during that awful time when she ached so with her broken heart.

With their help she got better over time, finally, and went to nursing school. When she met and married Roger Parkhill they visited less often, and when Cheryl came—wonderful, beautiful Cheryl—they went away completely. For years they stayed away, and she had actually forgotten about them, but then her beloved Cheryl left her, and this time they came back to stay. Night and day they had whispered to her over and over. Find a baby, they said, and make her your own. It didn't matter how or who she used, they told her.

Never very stable to begin with, Jeanine's thoughts had tumbled and clouded since Cheryl's death, and she had struggled and fought to keep her fragile grip on what sanity she had left. Now the struggle was over, and the only reality for her was the baby—her precious, wonderful baby. The companions tugged at her consciousness and swirled around her, merging into one commanding image and insisting that nothing else mattered.

Units from the Illinois State Police and the Chicago Police Department, accompanied by FBI agents, continued to follow Jeanine Boatman from a safe distance, and squad cars were stationed at strategic points along the Tri-State. It wasn't known if the woman was armed and they didn't want to put Rachel in danger. While the police weren't sure precisely where Jeanine was headed, they figured she'd stay on the tollway, and their plan was to take her at the tollbooth just north of Lake Cook. Roadblocks were in place and officers, including units called in from surrounding towns, were waiting to apprehend the woman. The net was set up so securely that as soon as Jeanine Boatman set foot out of the car she would be surrounded.

A couple of hours earlier, two Chicago police detectives, Frank Marszewski and Henry Adams, set up a post at the Ryland home to monitor the surveillance equipment set up in the living room, and listened to a police band radio that kept them updated on events. Clutching Rachel's pink bunny, Denise paced restlessly from room to room like a caged animal, stopping now and then in the living room to stare at the phone, willing it to ring, desperate for something—anything—to happen. The constant crackling of the police radio wore on her already frayed nerves, and she decided to join Jerry in the basement.

Jerry was a man who wasn't used to inactivity, and not being able to personally retrieve his child was driving him to the breaking point. Unable to concentrate on anything, he vented some of his frustration by working out. Denise came into his weight room and sat on the bench. He looked at her questioningly.

"Nothing," she said. "Still nothing."

"Damn. This is driving me nuts!" he said. He set his barbells down and wiped his face with the hem of his T-shirt.

Denise just shook her head sadly and sighed, dancing the little bunny on her knee.

"I know we're not supposed to give up hope," she said, "but it's so hard. I wish—"

Henry Adams called down the stairs. "Mrs. Ryland? Mr. Ryland? I think you folks better come up here."

Startled out of their despair, Denise and Jerry ran up the stairs two at a time. On the radio they heard police units talking back and forth about the trap they had set, coordinating themselves to close in on the kidnapper. Detective Marszewski was talking intently on his cell phone. At last, it looked as though they had finally and definitively tracked the kidnapper and would soon be able to take the her into custody. The time had come for action, and the two detectives, accompanied by Denise and Jerry, hurried to the squad car, heading for the scene of the proposed ambush.

So did Dale Romanski.

With its lights flashing and siren blaring, the squad car sped east across Golf Road, weaving in and out of the heavy traffic toward the Tri-State. Sitting in the back of the squad car, Denise's heart raced and she clutched Jerry's hand tightly. In her other hand she still held the stuffed bunny. Jerry leaned forward, urging Frank Marszewski to drive faster.

Each mile that passed brought the Rylands closer to the happy family reunion that had been little more than a dream for the past three days.

Unfortunately, the nightmare wasn't over yet.

31

Police and state troopers waited in tense anticipation at the tollway roadblock. So far, everything was going according to plan; Jeanine Boatman seemed to have no idea she was being followed, much less of the trap that lay ahead for her. All she had to do was keep driving, and they would have her.

In the often aggravating outcome of the best-laid plans of rodents and humans, this one came to ruin when they lost track of Jeanine's car. The police couldn't believe their rotten luck. Where had she gone?

Jeanine needed to tend to the baby, so she got off the tollway at Dundee Road in Northbrook and looked for a place to stop. She pulled into a McDonalds, and fed and changed the child and soothed her back to sleep. Hungry herself, Jeanine went through the drive-through and ordered the Chicken McNuggets that Cheryl had always liked, a large order of fries, and a large cola. Upon getting her food, she pulled into a space in the parking lot and ate, mildly interested in the sight of several police cars dashing by and oblivious to the idea that they might be looking for her.

The sight of the police cars made her think of the security she had provided for herself, and she opened the console between the bucket seats of her car to check on the small pistol she had stashed there. Jeanine gently touched the dull steel, as if for reassurance, and closed the console lid.

She finished eating and headed back toward the tollway, but as she neared the entrance ramp she changed her mind and decided instead to go west on Dundee to Highway 12. It would take longer to reach Lake Geneva that way, but it was a much more scenic route; it was such a beautiful day and she was so happy to have her darling with her. Jeanine glanced at the back seat, where the baby continued to sleep.

Jeanine Boatman's last-minute switch threw the police for a loop. The officers in the cars that had been following her and the ones that were posted ahead contacted each other, but no one had seen her. How in the hell, they wondered, had she managed to get past them, and how and where had they slipped up?

When the squad car carrying Denise and Jerry arrived at the tollbooth roadblock, they were greeted with the bad news. Dejected, Denise stayed in the squad car while Jerry got out and tried to find out what the next move would be. Just as she was about to get out and look for him, her cell phone rang. It was Romanski.

"I think I know where Jeanine Boatman's going," he said. "And I think I know how to pick up her trail. Wanna come along?"

Of course she did. Romanski told her he was just approaching the tollbooth, and to be waiting for him on the far-left side of the highway. He'd pick her up there.

"I think we'd better go it alone," he said. "She's bound to spook if she sees a bunch of cop cars coming."

She wasn't sure at first if she should do as he said. What about Jerry? How could she go off and leave him? Still, she trusted Romanski, and in her gut knew he was right. If she were to pull Jerry aside now and tell him what she was about to do, the police surely would overhear and then the trail might be lost. She had to leave Jerry behind.

"I'll be there," she told Romanski. She quickly jotted a note for Jerry and laid it on the back seat of the squad car, then slipped across the line of tollbooths to the side of the highway. About a minute later

Romanski's black Ford Taurus pulled up, and as he tossed coins in the toll basket she got in.

They turned around at Deerfield Road and backtracked to Dundee, where they proceeded west to Highway 12. Before long, Romanski pointed out a car traveling a few lengths ahead of them.

"That's her up ahead in the blue Honda," he said. Denise thought her heart would hammer through her chest.

"Do you know where she's going?" she asked, sure that he had done his homework and did indeed know. She wasn't disappointed by his answer.

"More than likely she's headed Lake Geneva, Wisconsin. She lived there with her grandparents after her parents died," he said. "It's a small town, and apparently she loves it there, so much so that she and Tucker even honeymooned there. Seems she's been house hunting there for weeks," he added.

"You're wonderful," she said, leaning over to kiss him on the cheek. "This is the most optimistic I've felt in almost three days. Thank you."

The gruff detective drove on, supposedly ignoring the kiss and never taking his eyes off the road, but a slight smile curled his lips.

Jeanine continued north toward Lake Geneva, grateful that there wasn't much traffic and that she was making good progress. She had the radio tuned to her favorite light-rock station and she sang love songs to the baby. Tucker had been a country music fan and had never let her listen to the music she liked while he was in the car. Well, she didn't have to worry about him anymore. She would make sure that her baby was exposed to all kinds of music, especially jazz, since it was the child's father's favorite.

As she neared the Wisconsin border the baby stirred and began fussing again. Jeanine sighed. They were less than an hour away from Lake Geneva and she had hoped she wouldn't have to stop until they got to the little bungalow on the edge of the town that would be their home. Thinking that the baby was probably wet though, she decided to stop. Besides, the soda she'd had at the McDonald's had caught up with her, and she badly needed to use a restroom.

"Okay, precious, Mommy's gonna stop now," she cooed to the baby as she pulled into a gas station near the town of Wauconda.

Still keeping a safe distance, Romanski slowly drove past the gas station, then stopped the car just on the other side. He leaned over and opened the glove box, revealing a pistol. He checked to make sure it was loaded, then slipped it into his jacket pocket.

"What now?" Denise asked. The sight of the gun had unnerved her.

"We're going to get your baby," he said. "We don't want her to see you, so stay here in the car and keep your head down."

She nodded and scooted down in the seat, staying just high enough to be able to see out the window. Romanski slipped out of the car and started edging toward the Honda.

As she watched him move away, Denise said a silent prayer. She was drenched in a cold sweat and felt as though she would fly into a million pieces any moment now. To just sit there waiting was exquisite torture; her baby was just a few yards away, and she longed to run to her. If anything were to go wrong now . . . But she trusted Romanski. She *had* to trust him.

"Be careful," she murmured, even though he was already out of earshot. "Bring my baby back to me."

Romanski crept around the back of the gas station and peered around the corner. Jeanine Boatman had made her trip to the ladies' room and now was coming out of the gas station and going back to her car, talking and cooing to the baby as she walked. As she opened the car door and started to put the infant back in the carseat, Romanski crouched low and, gun in hand, moved around the back of the car and edged to within inches of her. He reached out and was just about to grab her when a Lake County sheriff's deputy squealed up in a cloud of dust. He leaped from the car and leveled his revolver at Romanski.

"Freeze!" the deputy shouted.

Obediently, Romanski froze. Jeanine, alarmed, kept her hands on the baby in the car seat, and also froze. Then slowly she backed out of the car, clutching the infant. In the process, she opened the car console and slipped the pistol out, holding it hidden under the baby's blanket.

Denise, horrified at the terrible turn events were taking, jumped from the Taurus and ran across the gas station lot. Startled, the deputy turned his gun toward her and she froze.

"Officer, please," she cried. "You don't understand. That's my baby! That woman took my baby—"

"What the hell are you doing here?" Jeanine demanded, frantically trying to put all the shattered fragments together. Rachel, upset by the commotion, began to scream.

"Don't cry, sweetie!" Denise called to her upset child. "Mommy's here!"

"You're damned right," Jeanine sneered. "Mommy's here—right here!"

Totally confused, the deputy looked from one woman to the other.

"Lady, you just settle down now—and you too, lady." He turned to Romanski, who was still crouching beside the car. "And you put that gun on the ground and kick it over here," he commanded.

Romanski, whose knees were starting to give out in his awkward position, felt it was useless to try to explain and did as he was ordered. The deputy picked up the gun and tossed it in his squad car. Keeping his eyes on the group, he reached inside his car and called for back up.

Within moments two more deputies arrived, followed shortly after by state troopers and a contingent from Chicago PD, including the squad car carrying Detectives Marszewski and Adams and Jerry Ryland. Before the car had come to a complete stop, Jerry bolted from it and ran to Denise. Once he was sure she was all right he turned his attention to the woman holding his daughter. Showing no fear, she returned his gaze. Suddenly the fog lifted from her mind and she realized that the greatest irony of all stood before her and she began to laugh. It was time to tie up some loose ends.

32

While Detective Henry Adams kept an eye on Jeanine Boatman, Frank Marszewski explained the delicacy of the situation to the deputy who had been first on the scene. He in turn conferred with the other two deputies, and they all conferred with the state troopers. Finally, it was agreed that all the police would clear the area except for the first deputy and the two Chicago detectives. The troopers and deputies moved on and set up a perimeter guard, ensuring that if by some chance Jeanine Boatman managed to get away, she wouldn't get far.

Taking advantage of no longer being the center of attention, Romanski quietly edged further around the side of Jeanine's car. As things quieted down, the country sounds of humming cicadas and singing birds lent a surreal air to the scene.

The deputy kept his gun pointed at Jeanine. Denise and Jerry stood motionless as the woman holding their child willfully defied the lawman. Then Jerry spoke.

"Mrs. Boatman, I know it's been difficult for you since you lost your daughter. I know if I was in your shoes I'd be upset too." It took all his self-control to keep his voice low and calm. "But please, I beg you—don't hurt our baby. I promise you, if you just give us our baby we won't press charges. My wife is a lawyer and she can help you." He took a step closer. "Please, Mrs. Boatman, just give us our baby and we can all go home."

"Oh, trust me, I know your wife is a lawyer. She ruined my life. Because of her, *my* baby committed suicide." Jeanine's eyes glittered with hatred. "And don't talk to me about being in my shoes! How can you talk about being in my shoes after what you did to me?"

"Jerry, what is she talking about?" Denise said in a low voice.

"I have no idea," he answered. "I guess I'm confused, Mrs. Boatman, have we met before?"

"Have we met before?" she repeated, mocking him. "What a fool I am to think you'd remember."

Rachel cried pitiably and Jeanine rocked back and forth, trying to calm the baby.

"Funny how life twists and turns, isn't it, Jerry?" she said sarcastically. "So many coincidences that you can never predict. Oh, don't look so puzzled," she sneered. "I'm going to make it all crystal clear for you. We're going to have a little stroll down memory lane."

33

Jerry Ryland, the golden boy from southern California, was the starting halfback for the Memphis State Tigers. In good old Memphis, a town where a church, a liquor store, and now it seemed, a day care center shared every street corner, Jerry Ryland was on top of the world. An average student, he attended the university on an athletic scholarship. In his junior year, when Jerry had led the conference in rushing, his big dream was to finish his eligibility and then move on to the NFL. He would play for his beloved L.A., now St. Louis, Rams, following in the footsteps of James Harris and Lawrence McCutcheon, his childhood heroes.

In those days the great loves of his life were football, live jazz, and girls. He was a BMOC—big man on campus—and very popular with the young ladies. With his good looks and jazz guitar skills, he often found himself in the company of the prettiest female co-eds. Jerry may not have been the fastest guy on the team but there was one thing anyone who was around him quickly found out.

Jerry Ryland never gave up.

It was that dogged determination that first attracted the shy girl with glasses and frizzy blond hair to him. With her plain clothes and timid manner, she knew she was a far cry from the beautiful, outgoing girls he was always seen around, and even though the two of them were in a couple of classes together, he didn't seem to know she existed.

Jerry needed to play his senior year to give the NFL scouts another chance to evaluate him. He had always managed to maintain his academic eligibility, but in the past year his grades had started to slip, with chemistry giving him the biggest problem. His position coach suggested he try a tutor, and not wanting to lose the chance to play his senior season, Jerry agreed.

His academic advisor recommended an honor student, a sophomore who was in pre-med. She had always been a whiz at science and math, and the scientific theories that confused others were simple to her. She eagerly agreed to be Jerry's chemistry tutor.

Their first session together was awkward. Jerry had little understanding of chemistry and she was so in awe of him and being so close to him, she could barely concentrate. He was fascinatingly funny, a whole world apart from the dull boys she'd known in Wisconsin. Over time they got past their discomfort and with each tutoring session Jerry's understanding of the principles of chemistry increased while the girl's fondness for him grew.

Using the same tireless work ethic he showed on the gridiron, and with her gentle guidance, he studied hard and his grades improved. He passed the chemistry midterm exam with relative ease, and pulled an all-nighter studying for the final. Hopeful that his final grade would be a passing one, and knowing that he owed it to her if it was, he asked her to go with him to get it.

As he scanned the list posted outside the professor's door, she held his hand and she said a silent prayer.

And there it was: Not only had he passed the class, he got a B. Jerry would remain eligible to play football, and his dream of reaching the NFL was still alive. Elated, he whooped and picked her up and twirled her around, just like he did with the cheerleaders on the football field. Then he set her down and kissed her. It was the most wonderful moment of her life.

In gratitude, he invited her to go with him to a jazz concert at the Mid-South Coliseum that weekend, and she excitedly accepted. There was an added thrill in knowing how her grandparents would not approve of her dating an African American. In her best pink dress, and with her cheeks flushed and eyes sparkling, her plainness vanished and she looked very pretty. Jerry had borrowed a friend's car for the trip and when he picked her up, the shy girl from Lake Geneva, Wisconsin, and the handsome boy from southern California made a striking couple indeed.

The music at the concert was so romantic. She had never been a big jazz fan but she found herself having a great time regardless, and Jerry delighted in sharing his passion for the music with her. After the show they drove down Riverside Drive, where they parked and looked at the river and the lighted bridge. It was a cool spring night and he took off his jacket and draped it around her shoulders, then he went around to the trunk of the car and pulled out an old guitar. Jerry was an accomplished musician and she was amazed at how good he was when he began to play and sing "Close To You" to her.

They sat and talked a bit more. He told her how he had turned down music scholarships to Stanford and UCLA. The chance to play football was what had brought him to Memphis State and now, thanks to her, he'd be able to play for another year. They strolled along the banks of the Mississippi and he kissed her again. She had never felt like this before, so warm inside and tingly.

It grew late and they walked back to the car. He pulled her into the back seat and kissed and caressed her. Things progressed and she knew she shouldn't go so far. She had never done anything like that before, but she wanted him so badly. She vowed she would love him forever.

A few weeks later, school ended for the summer. She went back to Lake Geneva and Jerry went home to Los Angeles, and they promised to write each other. The pain of being away from him was almost unbearable, but there was nothing to be done about it. The days turned into weeks and the weeks turned into months, and all the while she never heard from Jerry Ryland. She sent dozens of letters and left countless phone messages, but he never returned her calls. What she didn't know was that three days after their romantic interlude, Jerry had met Denise Beaumont, who became the love of his life. He had forgotten about the mousy girl from Wisconsin as though she had never existed. That was when her companions returned, whispering around in her head as she slipped into a deep depression. Jeanine's worried grandparents sought help and the girl was diagnosed with mild schizophrenia. She began medication and improved significantly. However, she abandoned her dream of being a doctor and enrolled in nursing school at the University of Chicago.

A year after she graduated she met Roger Parkhill, an orderly at the Chicago General Hospital who was working his way through school with hopes of becoming a teacher. The marriage was a disaster; Roger was an alcoholic and unable to follow through on anything. The only good thing that came out of the marriage was Cheryl.

A few years after divorcing Parkhill, she met Tucker Boatman and she thought her life would be better. But he had turned out to be an abusive man with a criminal record, and she gave up hoping that she could ever love again. The only thing that had made her life worthwhile was her beautiful daughter, and even she had been taken from her.

Jeanine had never gotten over her first love, Jerry Ryland. In her dark moments she had often dreamed of what it would be like to have his child. Now she had her chance, and this baby would replace Cheryl. If Jeanine couldn't have Jerry, she could at least have a part of him—the best part. And to make it all sweeter, she would destroy the bitch lawyer who had ruined her life.

Just as Jeanine had told Jerry, real life is full of twists and turns that are stranger than any fiction. It was in one of those incredible turns that the person who had persecuted her and ruined her in the lawsuit she and Tucker had pressed against the Newville School Board was the wife of her one true love.

The money she received from the lawsuit had given her the means to achieve her goal. Poor, stupid Tucker had thought that she only wanted the baby, and agreed to help her if she would give him a half-million dollars. He then would leave and they could live their lives apart as they pleased. It was what they both wanted.

They had needed an accomplice, though, and Jeanine remembered the Richards woman after seeing her interviewed on television about her messy divorce. Jeanine's interest was piqued when she heard that Denise Ryland had represented Linda Richards' ex-husband. From the moment she first spoke with Linda over the phone, Jeanine knew she'd hit pay dirt. Linda was drooling for revenge, and when she heard the plan she was eager to go along. With her share of the money she could return to the five-star world she so desired.

Tucker worked part-time for the janitorial service that cleaned the building that housed Jerry's agency. He saw the notation on Jerry's calendar about the planned trip to California and Jeanine knew that the time to strike had come.

One of Tucker's friends, one with a criminal record as long as a July afternoon, worked at the airport. For five thousand dollars, he had acquired a flight attendant's uniform, a bogus aircraft access card, and a training manual with instructions on how to operate the equipment flight attendants were required to use. All they needed was to switch with someone on the crew. Linda Richards had assured Jeanine that it would be no problem to waylay flight attendant Cathy Thompson. Linda's hatred of Denise and her eagerness for revenge made convincing her to cut her long blond hair and dye it brown a snap.

Jeanine had offered Linda a half-million dollars to deliver the baby. Tucker had flown out to Los Angeles two days before and planted the stolen cars to be used for the trip down to San Diego. Jeanine had purchased the plane tickets for the return trip over the phone, and all Linda had to do was follow instructions.

Just as things were going well, the companions had come again, murmuring secrets to her of plots and schemes against her, and she grew too stubborn and troubled to take the medication she needed to control them. The companions told her what she had to do, and she surrendered to them. At their insistence she plunged ahead to the final, hateful ending.

She had the baby, and all she'd needed was to get rid of Linda and Tucker. Secretly offering each another half-million to kill the other, they greedily conceded. Now it was just her, her precious baby, and her companions.

Something was wrong now. This wasn't how it was supposed to turn out. Jerry was acting like he didn't know her.

"Jerry, it's me, Jeanie—Jeanie Archer. You must remember me," she said plaintively.

Jeanie Archer. The name rang a faint bell, but there was nothing familiar about the woman who stood before him. This was a woman who looked old and haggard, a woman to whom the years had not been kind.

"Jeanie . . ." he said slowly, "I'm sorry, I don't—"

"Shut up, Jerry!" she snapped. "Stop your faking. You're pretending you don't know me only because your precious little wifey is here. God forbid she should find out what hot lovers we were back in college."

Jeanie Archer. Jerry remembered a girl named Jeanie, but this old lady couldn't be her. Still, he knew he had to play along if he wanted to get his child back safely.

"Jeanie Archer," he said. "Sure, I remember you. But it's been a long time, and that's why—"

"Oh, stop it," Jeanine said. "I'm not interested in any of your pathetic excuses! I didn't need you then and I don't need your pity now! All I need is my baby!" The companions were right. She couldn't trust anyone. Whatever warm feelings she'd once had for Jerry Ryland were dead and gone.

Denise could stay quiet no longer. "Jeanine, whatever happened between you and Jerry was over long ago. I'm sorry if he hurt you, but that has nothing to do with my baby."

"*Your* baby! What about what you did to *my* baby?" Jeanine retorted.

"I can only imagine the pain you've endured," Denise said. "I'm sorry—I'm so very sorry. I never meant for any harm to come to your daughter, and I've regretted it ever since. You have to believe me. I was just doing my job."

"*Just doing your job*. Just because it's your job doesn't make it right! What you took from me I can never get back!" Jeanine shouted.

With each moment that passed she became more irrational and more agitated. The deputy from Lake County stood firm, his gun still pointed at the woman. Keeping out of Jeanine's line of vision, Dale Romanski edged closer.

With fury blazing in her eyes, Jeanine Boatman pulled the gun from under the baby's blanket and aimed it at Denise. It was a tense standoff. The deputy wasn't worried about being able to hit Jeanine at such a close range, but he wasn't sure if he could get her before she shot Denise. Besides, he didn't want to risk a shooting with the baby in the line of fire. The two detectives from Chicago PD motioned to him to hold his position.

Jeanine Boatman looked at the faces that surrounded her as the baby began to cry again. What had gone wrong? She had been a nurse and had spent her life helping people All she'd ever wanted in return was someone to love, a husband, a child. Was that so terrible?

There was the deputy, and the two policemen, pity and scorn on their faces. Who did they think they were to look at her like that? And Jerry, wimpy Jerry, condescending, pitying—treating her like she was some sort of pathetic animal.

Jeanine looked at Denise, whose eyes were intense and focused on her. It was because of her that everything had gone wrong, and the bitch was still ruining things. *Kill her*, the companions whispered, *killherkillherkillher* . . .

She started to squeeze the trigger and Romanski lunged. Jerry, fearing that Denise would be harmed, jumped in front of her. The young deputy saw his opportunity and fired at Jeanine, and as she fell to the ground her gun went off, striking Jerry in the shoulder.

"No!" Denise screamed as he spun and crumpled in her arms. A crimson stain blossomed across the front of his shirt.

Jeanine slumped to the ground, and Romanski grabbed the screaming baby and knocked the pistol from the woman's hand. Detective Adams rushed over, ready to handcuff her, but as she rolled over he saw that restraints would not be needed. A large wound gaped in her back, and blood was rapidly pooling beneath her.

"Get on the horn and get a couple of ambulances here in a hurry," he barked at the deputy.

Detective Marszewski went to Jerry's aid. Jerry lay unconscious and Denise cradled his head in her lap.

"Oh, Jerry, please, please don't leave me," she pleaded. "I need you, boyfriend. Rachel needs you."

His eyelids fluttered. "Denise? Baby, are you okay?" She nodded, tears glistening in her eyes. "What about the baby? Where's Rachel? Damn, that hurts!" he said as he tried sit up.

"Keep still, Mr. Ryland," Marszewski said. "I think your wound probably looks worse than it is, but no point taking chances. And here's your little girl."

Dale Romanski came over and handed the baby to her grateful parents. The infant howled her protest at the rough treatment she'd had.

Meanwhile, Henry Adams was doing what he could for they dying Jeanine Boatman.

"My baby," she wept. "Don't let them take my baby. She's all I have. Please . . ." The companions were gone now, and things were peaceful, so peaceful. "Cheryl?" she murmured as her eyes began to glaze. "Cheryl . . . wait . . ."

Sirens wailed as the ambulances pulled into the lot. Paramedics rushed to Jeanine's side, but time had run out for the woman who had once promised Jerry Ryland that only death would part them.

The medics focused their attention on Jerry, and once they were sure he was stable they loaded him onto a gurney and into an ambulance. Before she joined him, Denise turned to Dale Romanski.

"I don't know how I can ever thank you," she said, and again kissed him on the cheek.

"Hey, somebody's gotta pull your fat out of the fire," he said with a smile. He dusted himself off, and walked over and picked up his gun. "See ya back in the city, kiddo!"

Denise climbed into the ambulance with Jerry. She couldn't wait to nurse her baby. But just before the paramedic shut the ambulance door, Frank Marszewski carried something over and handed it to her. It was the little pink bunny.

As the ambulance pulled away, the exhausted but joyful parents marveled over their precious child, and as Denise cradled her treasure close, the baby's unhappy wails turned to soft gurgles and coos.

The wreckage had been enormous, but Denise Ryland realized that fair weather was in sight. The hurricane had blown itself out.